THE WINTER VISITOR

Nick parked his bicycle under the limp candy-striped awning and went inside. Behind the counter stood Mario, the proprietor, his hands on his hips.

'That the rain on again?' Mario served Nick with a packet of crisps. He inclined his head across the counter, lowered his voice. 'Had a bloke in an hour or so ago looking for your place. A stranger.'

'Oh?'

'He had your mother's name and address written on a piece of paper. Wanting a room I suppose. He had a suitcase with him, and one of those plastic flight bags.'

Nick shrugged. It *was* an odd time of year for someone to come looking for a room at the seaside but he was not going to say so.

'He had an Irish accent,' said Mario. 'But whether it was North or South I couldn't tell you. It's all one to me. Course you're part Irish yourself, aren't you?'

'Only a quarter. My grandmother's from Belfast.'

'Likely to be a connection of hers then.'

Also in Beaver by Joan Lingard

The Winter Visitor

Joan Lingard

Beaver Books

A Beaver Book

Published by Arrow Books Limited
17-21 Conway Street, London W1P 6JD

A division of the Hutchinson Publishing Group

London Melbourne Sydney Auckland
Johannesburg and agencies throughout
the world

First published in 1983
by Hamish Hamilton Children's Books
Garden House, 57-59 Long Acre, London WC2E 9JZ
Beaver edition 1984

© Copyright Joan Lingard 1983

Printed and bound in Great Britain by
Anchor Brendon Limited, Tiptree, Essex

ISBN 0 09 938590 2

For Robert, Rosalind and Henry

Chapter One

"Tell Mother I'll ring her later," said Andrea and hopped on the Edinburgh bus.

"She ain't going to like it," Nick sang out, but the automatic door was already folding shut behind her and the driver, who had seen her come running down the hill and waited, was now easing the bus out from the kerb.

Andrea rubbed a clear circle on the side window and waved. Although only her hand was visible Nick knew she would be smiling, not at him, but at her own secret thoughts. At least *she* imagined them to be secret. He considered it impossible not to know what his sister was up to.

The rear lights of the bus dwindled and were lost in the fast growing darkness. It had been a dark day, even for November, raining off and on, and they'd had the lights on in school. As Nick cycled off down the High Street he felt fresh spots of rain touch his face. He put on a spurt and before the drops had turned to a deluge had reached the Sea View Café on the corner of the promenade.

He parked his bicycle under the limp candy-striped awning and went inside. Behind the counter stood Mario, the proprietor, his hands on his hips, and at the corner table by the window sat two women – the only customers – drinking tea. The Sea View watchers, Nick's mother called them. Nothing much went past them, not if it was passing along the promenade. Little was of course in winter. From June to September it was different, with all the summer visitors around and cars standing bumper to bumper. Nick himself preferred the town in winter when the beach was deserted.

"That the rain on again then?" Mario served Nick with a packet of crisps. He inclined his head across the counter, lowered his voice. "Had a bloke in an hour or so ago looking for your place. A stranger."

"Oh?"

"He had your mother's name and address written on a

5

piece of paper. Wanting a room I suppose. He had a suitcase with him, and one of those plastic flight bags."

Nick shrugged. It *was* an odd time of year for someone to come looking for a room at the seaside but he was not going to say so with Mrs Plummer and Mrs Ramage listening. There was total quiet in their corner, without even the tinkle of a teaspoon to break it.

"He had an Irish accent," said Mario. "But whether it was North or South I couldn't tell you. It's all one to me. Course you're part Irish yourself, aren't you?"

"Only a quarter. My grandmother's from Belfast."

"Likely to be a connection of hers then."

Nick hoped not. He hoped too that his mother would have turned the man away. It was bad enough having to put up with other people in the house in summertime without having them in winter too.

He said he'd make a dash for it and left without looking at the women. The wet street glistened under the overhead lights, the sea was hidden behind a moving curtain of rain. He was drenched by the time he'd cycled the few yards down the rear lane to his house and put his bike in the shed. He went in through the back door to the kitchen.

The stranger was sitting in the armchair by the stove. He must have been asleep for as Nick entered his head jerked forward. He appeared confused, as if he could not remember where he was.

"Hello. I'm Nick Murray."

Before the man could say anything the door from the hall opened as though propelled by a gust of wind and Nick's mother came in.

"Thought I heard you! Nick, this is Ed Black. He's going to lodge with us for a day or two." She spoke very fast. Of course she would have had to leave her pupil to come through. She taught piano. To Mr Black she said, "This is Nick, my son."

The new lodger got to his feet to shake hands with Nick. He said he was very pleased to meet him and sounded as if he were not saying it merely out of politeness but as though

6

he really meant it. Nick could not see why he should. The man stood awkwardly, his weight unevenly balanced, leaning a little to the right.

"Mr Black's been in an accident and is convalescing," said Mrs Murray. "I'd better get back to my pupil." But she did not go. She fiddled with her belt, tucked a piece of hair back behind her ear. Nick watched her hands.

Why was she so nervous? *Was* the man connected to her family in some way? Though presumably if he were she would have said so at the start. Or would she? She didn't like talking about her relatives in Belfast.

"Oh by the way, Mum, Andrea asked me to tell you she's gone to Edinburgh to see Janey." He waited for her outburst. None came. She nodded absentmindedly and said, "Perhaps you'd like to make Mr Black a cup of coffee?" and left.

Nick put the kettle under the tap and whilst he waited for it to fill looked through the wet window at the black and yellow tree in the middle of the garden. The leaves were going, a few more puffs of wind, a few more heavy showers, and they would all be gone. He must paint the tree before it took on its winter aspect. He would do it on Saturday, the day after tomorrow.

"You don't need to trouble, you know," said the man, making Nick jump. For a moment he had forgotten him.

"No trouble. I could be doing with a cup myself." He lit the gas and set the kettle on the flame.

Ed Black sat down again stretching his right leg out in front as he lowered himself. He didn't look at all well: his face was thin, his eyes sunken. Filled out, he would be a strong, handsome looking man.

"Was it a car accident?"

"No." Ed Black hesitated, then said, "A bomb went off under my heels."

"Oh." What else did one say to someone who had narrowly escaped being blown up? You couldn't very well ask for details. Nick waited. He saw pain in the man's eyes and turned away to attend to the steaming kettle. "Milk and sugar?"

"Please."

"Biscuit?"

"No thanks. Your mother very kindly gave me some sandwiches when I arrived."

Nick drank his coffee, trying not to stare at the man over the rim of the mug. There did seem to be something odd about his coming here, though he could not put his finger on what exactly it was.

"You don't know my grandmother, do you by any chance?"

"Your grandmother?" He looked confused. "I don't think –"

"It's all right, I just wondered. She's from Belfast, that's all. She lived there until she came over to Scotland to marry my grandfather."

"I see. Is he still alive?"

"No. But she is." Nick smiled to himself.

The rain suddenly increased in tempo and began to flail the window. Ed Black made a comment on the wildness of the day.

"You'd have been better off going to Majorca to convalesce," said Nick. "Wind comes straight off the North Sea here in winter."

"I couldn't afford Majorca. Besides, I like wild weather."

"So do I!"

"That's something we have in common then."

Nick drew back a little. Why would a stranger talk about having things in common? Especially when he only intended to stay for a few days.

"What made you come over to Scotland?"

"I wanted out of Northern Ireland. Well, after what happened . . ."

Nick nodded.

Mrs Murray returned, having dismissed her last pupil of the day. "Now I've got time to show you your room. Would you like to come this way?"

The lodger picked up his suitcase and flight bag, refusing Nick's offer of help, saying he could manage. There was a

8

choice of rooms, said Mrs Murray, as she led the way, since it was out of season. Two rooms on the first floor were vacant and two on the top. He would choose the top, thought Nick, for that was more private. And in spite of the talk about having things in common, Ed Black wanted to be private, you could tell that at a glance; secretive even. He looked like a man who wanted to hole up somewhere.

No one else slept on the top floor in winter. Nick and his mother and Andrea all slept on the first floor. And their father, when he was home. He was in the Persian Gulf at present, working as a chef for a gas liquefaction plant. Nick had found it strangely difficult to think about his father since he had gone. Perhaps it was the distance. Or because he couldn't imagine what it would be like in the Gulf. He didn't know.

Or perhaps it was because he was enjoying the peace in the house and felt guilty that he should. Before his father went he and his mother had been clashing a lot, quarrelling, making-up, then arguing again. Nick hated quarrels, whereas Andrea thrived on them. She said they added spice to life. She said, too, that he took life too seriously.

He lifted a pencil and idly began to draw Ed Black's face on the inside cover of his homework notebook.

His mother came back saying she must get their meal on.

"Is he going to eat with us?"

"No. Just bed and breakfast."

"Did he put down a deposit?"

"I didn't ask him to. I prefer to trust people."

Instead of going to the cooker she began to pick up things and move them around the room. It was her form of tidying. She looked preoccupied. Wisps of fair hair had escaped from the French knot on the nape of her neck adding to her look of absentmindedness.

"He wasn't a friend of your Uncle George's, was he?"

"Uncle George?" The pin box she was holding slipped from her hand and dozens of small spiky pins cascaded on to the thick pile hearth rug where they proceeded to embed themselves. Nick went down on his knees and started to pluck them out one by one. "Of course not," she said. "Why should he be?" She sounded distressed.

"I just wondered where he'd got our address from, that's all."

"It could hardly have been from Uncle George, could it? He's been dead a long time."

"Yes, he has, hasn't he?" Nick sucked blood from the tips of his fingers. "So why do you get so upset when his name's mentioned?"

"I don't! Well maybe I do a little . . . It was the *way* he died."

"But you didn't like him, did you?"

"That doesn't mean I was glad that he was shot!"

Nick picked up the last pin and laid it in its box. He frowned down at the rows of shiny pins. His Great-Uncle George, whom he did not remember, had been shot on his doorstep in Belfast by the IRA in 1970. He had been in some sort of Protestant paramilitary organisation, according to his mother, although his grandmother – George's sister – strongly denied it. George wouldn't have hurt a fly, she maintained. Once the two women had been on the verge of a row about it and then his mother had backed off saying there wasn't much point in raking up the past now and changed the subject.

"Surely you don't think that, Nick?"

"No, of course not. Anyway, how *did* Mr Black get our address?"

"You remember the Simpsons from Belfast? They were here in the summer. They told him about us." Nick went to fetch his magnet.

They ate alone together. Mrs Murray was quiet. She didn't even cross-question him about Andrea. The coming of the Northern Irish man had certainly disturbed her.

Ed Black bought his meal at the chip shop, a white pudding supper. A full report was given to Nick later when he went to buy milk for his mother.

"Not a very talkative man," complained Toni, who was Mario's brother. He had another brother too, called Carlo, who was in business in Edinburgh. "Salt and sauce. That was all I could get out of him. Polite enough though. Funny like coming here in November." Toni turned over the chips in the steaming fat and yawned, patting his mouth with the back of his free hand. "Your mother should watch who she takes in. Her being on her own."

Nick protested.

"Well, with your father away, I mean. There's some who are always ready to take advantage of a situation like that. Good looking woman, your mother."

Nick supposed she was, though he had never given much thought to it. Nor did he wish to discuss the subject with Toni who was in no hurry to pass over the milk.

"How's Mr Murray liking his new job?"

"Well enough."

"Must be pretty hot out there. Not like here," said Toni mournfully. He closed the shop once a year for a fortnight and went to Italy. To get warm, he said. "Your Andrea still seeing our Carlo?"

"I think so. I'll just get the milk myself, shall I?" Nick went round the back of the counter.

"I've told Carlo to lay off. 'She's too young for you', I said to him, but he doesn't listen to what I say. What have *I* got?" Tony stabbed his white coat with his forefinger. "Only a chip shop at the seaside. *He* has a smart restaurant in Edinburgh. *He* has customers all year round."

"Yes, well . . ." Nick backed away, clutching the pint of milk to his chest. He had enough of family squabbles without hearing about other people's.

He walked along the High Street, passing the Sea View Café which was now closed, and went down the steps on to the wet sands. The tide was coming in, he could see the froth of the sea through the dark rain. He felt the spray on his face.

Turning his back to the sea, he surveyed the street and its houses. He would like to paint the terrace at night. Rectangles of light broke the dark, larger rectangle of the terrace into patterns. Some people always drew their curtains; others did not. Mrs Plummer at number three was one of those who never did: she sat well placed in her room, watching the television set with one eye and the road outside with the other. As he watched he saw her short body come towards the window and her moon-shaped face swim into view. She peered out into the night. She would see nothing but the rain which was thinning to a mist and the sodden bushes in her narrow front garden. *He* was invisible. The knowledge pleased him.

Mrs Plummer was a piano teacher, like his mother. Mrs Plummer hated his mother. Mrs Plummer had been teaching the piano to children in this town for twenty-five years and there was nothing she didn't know about teaching the piano except how to keep pupils. Any she did get she soon lost. They gradually moved two doors further up the street. His mother now had more pupils than she could cope with and Mrs Plummer had too much time to spend standing at her window.

She went back to her chair beside the fire.

The window on the top floor of number seven, his own house, was also lit and uncurtained, and the edge of a man's profile could be seen. He, too, would be able to watch the street. He would have a good view. A sea view. Was it the sea he wanted to watch? What was *he* doing here?

The window below was lit but curtained. This was Nick's mother's room. It was like a cave, with lights set low, full of colour and textures, and warmth. The thought of warmth pulled him away from the sea and back towards the house.

As he opened the front door the telephone on the hall table started to ring. He lifted the receiver.

The caller was Andrea. She sounded as if she had been drinking, which she might well have been, in the chrome-plated cocktail bar of Carlo's restaurant. He thought he could hear restaurant sounds in the background. She was going to spend the night at Janey's, she said, and would get the bus in to school in the morning. "Will you tell Mother?"

"Why don't you tell her yourself?" said Nick irritably. "Why should I do your dirty work for you?"

"I don't want to disturb her."

12

"That's very considerate of you," he said, laying on the sarcasm. "And how is Carlo? Dearest Carlo?"

"Oh do shut up! You can be such a pain in the neck!"

"If you need any assistance with his bath chair just let me know."

With that remark, he put down the receiver, quietly, then lifted it off again and laid it on the table for a minute so that if she tried to re-dial she would get the engaged sound. She would be furious, she couldn't stand not getting the last word. He smiled. Infantile, that's what his mother would call their exchange.

He went upstairs whistling.

"Nick, you're soaking. That's the second time today! Come in to the fire. You'll be coughing again tonight."

"So I'll be coughing. That was Andrea on the phone."

"Staying with Janey?"

"Yes."

"I might have known. And seeing Carlo – you don't have to tell me! He's really quite unsuitable for her. In every way." Mrs Murray sighed. "What is he – ten, eleven years older than her?"

"Twelve."

"She won't listen to me, Nick, you know she won't. I feel so helpless. If your father was here it might be different."

"She'll be eighteen at Easter."

"That's not very old. She's got this year to finish at school and then three or four at university . . . "

"She's not talking about getting married."

"I hope not! She hasn't said anything to you has she?"

"Not a word," said Nick, watching the steam rise like mist from the legs of his jeans. "Of course she wouldn't tell me even if she were." She kept her confidences for Janey or her school friend Mandy. To both she gabbled into the phone for hours. He wondered that they didn't bore themselves into a state of paralysis.

Overhead, the Irishman moved. Nick and his mother cocked their heads, listened. The board's creaked, a door opened, and the lodger's feet descended the stairs to bring

13

him down to their level. For a moment he paused, listening too perhaps, and everything was quiet, except for the crackling and sparking of the logs in the fire-place. Then he went into the bathroom.

"Is he Protestant or Catholic do you think?" asked Nick.

"I don't know. And I don't care." His mother's voice was sharp.

"Gran can always tell, at least she says she can. Do you think she can?"

"I daresay. It's the kind of thing she's interested in certainly. But I, Nick, am not!"

"All right, keep your hair on! I was only wondering. How do you think she can tell though?"

"Facial types. I suppose. Names."

"Can't tell much from Ed Black can you? Pretty neutral sort of name that."

The bathroom door opened and he came out again. He was coughing. It was a short, hacking cough. He coughed all the way back up the stairs.

"Don't bother mentioning him to your grandmother by the way, in case she rings up. Well, you know what she's like . . . We don't want her coming out here to give him the third degree."

Nick was still sitting over his second cup of coffee when the lodger came down in the morning.

"Hope I'm not late?"

"Not at all," said Mrs Murray. "There's no hurry. I don't teach in the mornings. Except for Saturdays. Bacon and egg?"

"Yes please"

"I wish *you*'d eat something, Nick."

"I'm not hungry."

She shook her head and began peeling off strips of bacon to lay under the grill.

"I see another soldier was shot on foot patrol in Belfast yesterday," said Nick, looking up from the paper.

"Yes, it's terrible." Ed Black's words were flat, and unemotional; he was not going to give anything away.

"It's time you were off, Nick," said his mother. "You'll be late if you're not careful."

He didn't really care if he was late, he wouldn't care if he didn't go to school at all. It was not that he hated it or anything like that; he just couldn't be bothered with it. He could think of better ways to spend his time.

"Nick –"

"I'm going!"

"See you later," said Ed Black.

As Nick wheeled his bicycle out of the shed he got a strong whiff of the cooking bacon and felt suddenly intensely hungry. Saliva ran in his mouth. He stopped off at Mario's and bought a packet of smoky bacon crisps. Mario was just opening for the day.

"So how's the lodger?"

"All right, as lodgers go."

"Not a long lost cousin then?"

"No."

Nick left the café and the sea and cycled slowly along the High Street and up the hill towards the school. He rode with one hand on the handlebars and with the other ate the crisps from his pocket. A few pupils were still making their way up the hill though most would already be inside the playground milling about waiting for the bell to ring. As he neared the top, a long low red car swept out of a side street and screeched to a halt outside the school gates. Nick put his foot down on the kerb and halted.

Andrea got out of the car, her long fair hair falling across her face as she bent down to say goodbye to the driver. Then the school bell began to ring, making enough noise to split your skull in two. Andrea slammed the car door, waved, and clutching her books under her arm ran in through the gates. He had better move himself. The last-minute Murrays, that was what they were called by his form teacher, who said he couldn't understand why, for it wasn't as if they had far to come, unlike some pupils who

15

lived right out in the country. Nick's friend Joe Marks was one of those, and yet he was always on time, early, in fact; he couldn't bear to lie in bed, was up at first light, out in the open air messing around with his various bits and pieces of machinery. He was rebuilding a Mini from the wreck of an old one. Scorning the school bus, he cycled the eight miles in and out to school every day, winter and summer. He liked to have his own wheels under him.

The red car did a U-turn and headed for the Edinburgh road. Crunching the last of his crisps, Nick watched it go.

A piercing whistle roused him. Looking back at the school gate, he saw Joe signalling to him.

"Come on, Rembrandt! Get some steam up!"

As Nick went whizzing in through the gates, Joe brought his arm down like a marshal lowering the chequered flag at a motor race.

Chapter Two

"I've decided to save for a scooter," said Joe at the morning break, as they jogged down the hill to the small shop that served as a kind of tuck shop for the school.

"I thought you wanted to put all your money into parts for the car?"

"Yeah, well I do, but I want a bit of power under me *now* as well." Joe grinned. "It'll be a year before I can get the car on the road. Or be able to drive it legally anyway. And the bike's getting a bit slow." He was sixteen, a year older than Nick, though they were in the same class. He'd got a bit behind with his schooling as his parents were forever moving on.

"How's the work scene?"

"Got a couple of car services lined up. And logs to saw."

An enormous queue snaked out of the shop along the pavement. They joined the back of it.

"Wish there was some way I could earn money," said Nick.

"You will one of these days, Rembrandt. When you're famous. I'll be able to brag about knowing you."

"That'll be the day!"

They shuffled along, reached the doorway. Pupils carrying cans and bags pushed past on their way out.

"Hey, there's Katy McIlroy up front!" said Joe.

Craning his neck, Nick saw the girl's dark head at the counter.

"Get us a couple of Cokes would you, Katy?" Joe called out.

"Okay, Joe."

"Want some money? Catch!"

He threw a fifty pence piece over the waiting heads.

"Not fair," muttered one or two, but not too loudly. Nobody would want to take on Joe Marks. Besides, he was popular.

Nick and Joe retreated to the pavement where they waited, stamping their feet to keep warm.

With arms full of cans of Coke and various bags, Katy appeared, followed by two friends, both smaller than she, one red-haired, the other fair. She herself was tall and thin, with black fizzy hair which she tossed around a great deal. She was a vivacious girl, seldom still, and she had a high, infectious laugh. Nick didn't know any of the girls, except by sight, for they were all in the year below him and Joe.

"Thanks, Kit-Kat," said Joe. "Saved our lives."

She blushed, met his eyes, looked away.

"Hello, Nick," she said, very friendly, turning to him, surprising him, for he hadn't even known that she would know his name. It was the first time she had ever spoken to him.

"Hello." He gave a vague nod in the direction of the other two.

The bell was ringing, summoning them back. They moved off in a bunch but gradually Katy and Joe surged ahead and Nick found himself between the other two girls. It just seemed to happen, without him being aware that it was. He watched the backs of Joe and Katy who walked close together, their elbows bumping. They seemed to have plenty to talk about, and laugh about.

He had no idea what to talk to these two girls about. They covered a few yards in silence and then the fair-haired one broke it saying, "Turned colder, hasn't it?"

"Yes," he said, quickening his step and lengthening his stride, wishing they would hurry up too. The gap was widening between them and the pair in front. The bell was still ringing. "It's better than rain, I suppose," he added, feeling foolish, for discussions of the weather did not interest him at all.

"The forecast said there might be snow at the weekend," said the red-haired girl. "At least on high ground," she finished up limply.

"Was there much out your way last time?" asked Nick, not sure which way that was, but he had a vague idea that Katy McIlroy lived out of town, and because she did they probably did too.

"I live just along the road from you."

"Oh yes, so you do." Of course she did! She lived at the other end of the terrace. What an idiot she must think he was!

"I get lessons from your mother."

The fair-haired girl giggled.

His mother often said he was observant only when he wanted to be, and that when he didn't he was as blind as a bat in a snowstorm.

The bell ceased and the air seemed suddenly intensely quiet.

"Come on, Rembrandt," shouted Joe, turning round and walking backwards, "or you'll be late again."

At lunchtime Mrs Murray was preoccupied with the subject of his lateness, and Andrea's. She was frowning over a letter which she had received from the school.

"Why *are* you late so often, Nick? I don't understand it. I know only too well why Andrea is and I'll have to put my foot down about this staying with Janey during the week but you go out in plenty of time."

He made a face.

"You can't go on like this."

"Okay, don't start!"

She did of course and having started went on to tell him how fed up she was and that it was *she* who got the letters and was made to feel responsible but at his age it was time he took over the responsibility himself. When she paused he said he was sorry and would try to mend his ways.

"I don't mean to be late. I get – well – sidetracked."

"I know," she said, calm now. They grinned at one another.

"Just try to keep your mind on getting there, will you?"

"Okay, I'll try. Joe's coming down, is that all right? I asked him in for some soup, it was so cold."

"Of course. Any time, you know that."

Joe arrived in good spirits. He had stopped off to have a word with Katy McIlroy. That girl had suddenly started to appear everywhere, thought Nick. Turn your head and there she was, flanked by the two attendants. Joe talked to

19

Mrs Murray whilst she put the finishing touches to the soup and cut up a crusty French loaf. She liked Joe. She liked his good humour, and the way he made an effort to talk to her. More than Nick did for Joe's mother. But Mrs Marks didn't seem to mind and would give him a commentary on her week's doings without expecting much contribution from him in return.

"No sign of Andrea?" asked Mrs Murray.

Nick had seen her heading for a café further up the town with Mandy. They spent most of their lunchtimes in there drinking coffee and smoking cigarettes. He didn't tell his mother about the smoking, though he suspected that she knew.

"I wish she'd come home for lunch."

"She doesn't know what she's missing," said Joe, eyeing the pot of soup.

"Where's the lodger?" asked Nick.

"Gone for a walk, I think." They heard the front door opening. "Sounds like him now. What about asking him to join us for some soup?"

Nick hesitated. He didn't feel much like asking the lodger to join them – once he started having meals with them he'd be in the kitchen all the time – but he didn't like to say so in front of Joe. He got up and intercepted Ed Black at the foot of the stairs and made the offer which was accepted at once.

"This is very good of you," the lodger said as he came into the kitchen. "Are you sure you have enough now?"

Mrs Murray nodded and smiled and began to ladle out the lentil soup. Nick introduced Joe and Ed who got into conversation about cars. Mrs Murray listened, inserting the odd question, but Nick's mind drifted away. He was thinking of how the waves looked when they were on the brink of curling and breaking and how difficult it was to capture that exact moment in paint. He had tried several times, would try again.

"Nick, more soup?" his mother was asking.

"No thanks."

Joe and Ed finished the pot for her. She wanted it

finished, she said, as she dumped it in the sink and ran in cold water; that way she could make a different kind tomorrow.

"My mum hates making soup," said Joe cheerfully. "So it's cans and packets for us most of the time."

"You don't look as if you're fading away on it, Joe," said Mrs Murray.

He laughed.

Nice lad that, she would say to Nick later, I don't know why you don't spend more time with him. Because he lives too far away, that's why, he would answer. They had the same conversation every time Joe came to the house. Funny the way people kept repeating themselves. He suspected that his mother felt he was safe when he was with Joe. Joe had a kind of solid feel to him that gave people confidence. You couldn't imagine him in a panic, confused, his back against the wall. But was that true? Everybody had their bad moments.

"You're from Belfast then?" Joe was saying to Ed. "Did you leave because of the Troubles?"

"I suppose, in a way." He was not going to elaborate.

"Are you going back?"

"Probably not."

"Coffee, boys, before you go?" said Mrs Murray, breaking in.

"What do you think of him then?" asked Nick on their way back to school.

"Seems a nice enough guy."

"He's guarded though, don't you think?"

"Guarded?"

"It's like a shutter comes down at the back of his eyes at times."

"Like you, when you turn off?"

"No, not like that," said Nick, but Joe only laughed and wasn't interested in carrying the conversation further. He would take Ed Black, as he took other people, as he found him, and not look for complications.

Andrea was home before Nick in the afternoon. She had a free period last thing Friday and since she was in the Sixth Year she did not have to stay in school. She was drinking coffee in the kitchen, dressed in a scarlet combat suit with black boots.

"Where are you going? As if I need ask! Why don't you go and live in Edinburgh?"

"I wish I could. There's nothing going on in this dump."

Their mother was teaching. They could hear the plodding notes of a child moving up and down the scale.

"Does she know you're going out again?"

"Haven't seen her yet."

"We've got a lodger by the way."

"A lodger?" That raised Andrea's eyebrow. "At this time of year?"

Nick told her everything he knew about Ed Black, which was not much. Andrea was only mildly interested. After all, she was seldom at home, as Nick pointed out, and as their mother pointed out too when she finished her lesson and came to have a quick cup of coffee.

"You'd think you were a lodger here yourself, Andrea. Only you don't pay and you don't always come home at night."

Nick got out his sketch book and began to draw the tree in the back garden. The usual arguments were about to begin.

"I'm seventeen and *three*-quarters now, Mother, you seem to forget that. You've got to accept that I'm old enough to lead my own life."

"Except that you can't pay for it yet."

"All right, if that's what you want, I'll leave school and get a job."

"Doing what?" murmured Nick. "There are three million unemployed."

Andrea ignored him. Her cheeks were almost as red as her suit and she had her hair tossed back over her shoulder. She faced her mother. "It might be better if I did get a job.

22

Then I could pay for a room in a flat in Edinburgh."

She had no intention of doing that, Nick knew, but she spoke with passion and conviction as if she really believed it herself, and his mother, who also knew that Andrea did not mean it, rose to the bait and took it.

"Go ahead then," she said, her anger mounting, "if that's what you want!"

They had a few more rounds and then their mother crumpled into a chair burying her face in her hands. She couldn't take many more of these rows, she said; they drained her. Nick stabbed his pencil point into the table and glared at Andrea. But she was already repenting and had her arms round her mother's shoulders saying she was sorry, she hadn't meant it, she hadn't wanted to hurt her and she wouldn't leave home. All very exhausting, thought Nick, just to come back to the point at which they had begun. The two women made up, half-laughing, half-crying, and then the next pupil was ringing the door bell.

"No peace for the wicked," said Nick, getting up. "I'd better go since you two look the worse for wear."

He opened the door to Katy McIlroy's fair-haired friend.

"Hello," she said, stepping into the hall carrying her music case in her hand.

"I didn't know you had lessons too."

"I've just started up with your mother. I used to go to Mrs Plummer."

"Just go in," he said, opening the door for her, not looking at her face as she passed.

"Now you're *not* to be too late tonight," his mother was saying to Andrea when he returned. "Promise! And you're not to ring up and say you're staying at Janey's. I'd like you under my roof for a change."

Andrea promised and kissed her mother.

"Will Carlo be driving you home?"

"I expect so."

"I hope he doesn't drive too fast?" said Mrs Murray anxiously.

"No Mother, he doesn't. He drives —"

"Like a slug," finished Nick.

"Nick!" said his mother. "You can be so –"

"Exasperating. I know. Your pupil's in."

"I must go. See you later, dear," she said to Andrea and went.

Andrea got her jumble-sale fur coat out of the cupboard and pulled it on.

"It's a wonder Carlo doesn't buy you a mink," said Nick and ducked as she took a swing at him. She was a strong girl, played hockey for the First Eleven and captained the girls' fencing team.

"I'd better go or I'll miss my bus. Couldn't lend me a pound could you?"

"A pound? Me?"

"Fifty p. then. I haven't got enough for the bus. I was going to ask Mum but I can't now."

Grumbling, he fished fifty pence out of his pocket.

"Thanks. I'll pay you back."

"Don't forget," he shouted after her. But she was gone, like a whirlwind, with the moth-eaten fur flying out behind her.

The fair-haired girl was playing a piece by Mozart. Pretty ghastly rendering it was too, he thought, and closed the door into the hall. In the kitchen peace reigned. He went back to his tree.

Chapter Three

Saturday morning. Nick stood with his back to the kitchen painting the black and yellow tree. Behind him Andrea was going on about the lodger. In spite of her promise she had come home very late last night and she and her mother had already had a row about that, so now she was determined to be the one to find fault.

"Seems very odd if you ask me just arriving like that out of the blue. It's a bit of a risk taking him in when you know nothing about him."

"He's a friend of the Simpsons," said Nick, without moving his head.

"What do I ever know about paying guests?" said Mrs Murray.

"They usually write in advance, from addresses," said Andrea.

"So he didn't write. I can't see that it matters much."

"You never know what he might be up to."

"You sound just like Mrs Plummer."

That blunted Andrea, which it had been calculated to do.

"Eat up your breakfast before it gets cold," said Mrs Murray. "And I wish you'd eat something too, Nick."

He said that he would, in a minute, and went on mixing cadmium orange with yellow ochre. A gust of wind, and half of the leaves would be away. Their hold on the tree was precarious.

Andrea muttered something about London bombings to which her mother replied that they were a long way from London, and men on wanted lists were more likely to conceal themselves in the anonymity of the city rather than an empty seaside resort in winter where the inhabitants were more vigilant than MI5.

"It would be a terrible world if we were all to become suspicious of everybody else. Just because he's from Northern Ireland!"

"I don't know why we have to go on taking p.g.s, now that Dad's earning all that money."

"He hasn't been earning it all that long," her mother reminded her. "And we had a few years before it when he didn't earn anything at all, don't forget."

"That wasn't his fault," said Andrea, flaring. "Lots of people can't get jobs these days."

"He had jobs, he just couldn't keep them."

"That's not fair!"

Nick wished that Andrea would hurry up and eat her breakfast and go back to Edinburgh where she – and he – wished she belonged.

Mrs Murray said that her remark had been perfectly fair: their father had been in and out of more jobs in the last ten years than she could count on the fingers of both hands. Please don't bother to count them, said Nick in his head. He knew that what she said was true but his father *was* trying now. At least he hoped he was.

Their argument was terminated by the arrival of the lodger who hesitated in the doorway looking as if he felt unsure about intruding on the family.

"Come in," said Mrs Murray, clearing a space on the table by pushing tubes of paint, pieces of turpentined rag and disengaged pages of the *Scotsman* to one side. "I don't believe you've met my daughter Andrea yet?"

He and Andrea shook hands and when Nick took a quick glance over his shoulder he saw that his sister had ceased to look sullen and was wearing that smile which she considered to be alluring.

Ed Black came and stood behind Nick. He looked at the tree taking shape on the easel, then at the tree in the garden. He nodded.

"You've got it all right."

The words of praise pleased Nick for he felt that Ed Black was not the kind of man who would say things just for the sake of it. "Thanks," he mumbled.

"Going to be a painter when you leave school?"

"Hope so."

"Difficult life, eh?"

"No more than many others these days," said Mrs Murray.

"You're right there." Ed Black turned.

"And what do you do, Mr Black?" asked Andrea.

"I'm a mechanical engineer. And what about yourself?"

"I want to be a microbiologist."

"Indeed? That's interesting."

"*If* you get enough A levels," said Mrs Murray. She had the bacon packet in her hand and was looking at the lodger. "Same as yesterday?"

"Yes, please."

Andrea removed a pile of laundry from the chair so that he could sit down. "Family life! Have you much experience of family life, Mr Black?"

If she could hear herself! thought Nick.

"Only when I was younger."

"Were you one of a large family?"

"Reasonably."

Nick grinned. This man was an expert at giving non-committal answers.

Their mother was making a lot of noise slapping the grillpan about and clattering crockery. Andrea continued to make inquiries about the lodger's family, wanting to know how many, what sex and age. He revealed that he had two brothers and two sisters and his father was dead. In a remarkably short time Mrs Murray produced a plateful of bacon and eggs, only one of which was broken, and two fried potato scones.

"Ah, potato bread," said Ed Black. "Fantastic!"

"That's what our grandmother calls it. Not scones," said Andrea. "She's from Belfast too, of course."

"So I believe."

"Perhaps you'll meet her while you're here."

"It's not very likely," said Mrs Murray. "Mr Black's going on Monday."

That wasn't a very long stay, said Andrea, not really long enough in which to convalesce was it? He thought he might visit some friends in the north of England after he left here, he told her.

"Which part of Belfast are you from?" she went on, relentlessly. She would have been good at the Inquisition, thought Nick. "Our grandmother's from East Belfast."

"West."

"And never the twain shall meet," said Nick softly, catching Andrea's eye.

She gave him a look that was meant to convey contempt and then the telephone rang giving them what Nick considered to be a merciful release. She would shiver in the hall for the next half hour. He even allowed his mother to persuade him to stop painting for ten minutes and eat a bacon sandwich and drink a cup of coffee. He sat at the table beside the lodger.

"Are you going to stay in England?"

"I'm hoping to go to America. I've got relatives in Baltimore."

Ed Black was not going to reveal any more; he picked up the paper and through streaks of yellow and orange paint began to read the world's news. Nick observed that when he read a report from Ulster his face took on a blank look. He showed no reaction whatsoever. Odd that. Unless . . .

The doorbell rang.

"That'll be Mario's daughter," said Mrs Murray. "Go and let her in, Nick, would you please?"

Marcellina was waiting in the front porch, her piece of music under her arm, her black pigtails twisted tight, her white knee socks gleaming, looking as if ice cream wouldn't melt in her mouth. When playing in the back alley she screeched like a banshee.

"In you go," said Nick, opening the door of the music room. Marcellina went in, the emerald green ribbons at the end of her pigtails bobbing.

As he was about to close the front door he saw a red car rounding the corner by the Sea View Café.

"Here's lover boy coming," he called over his shoulder to Andrea who said a hasty goodbye to Mandy and jumped up to examine herself in front of the mirror. She pulled back her shoulders, flicking her hair behind them.

The car stopped at the gate and Carlo emerged bent in two like a half-shut knife. He was tall for an Italian, much taller than his two older brothers Mario and Toni who were not only short but inclined to stoutness. Carlo straightened himself out and brushed off the shoulders of his blue velvet jacket. Under it he wore a striped silk shirt. Everything about him shone: his jacket, his shirt, his hair, his smile.

"Good morning, Nick," he called. "And how are you this morning?" But he was not really interested, he was already looking past him, at Andrea.

Nick left them to it and went back to the kitchen where the lodger was washing the dishes.

"You don't have to, you know," Mrs Murray was saying as she prepared to depart to give her lesson to Marcellina.

"I know that. But I don't mind washing dishes. And I haven't much else to do."

"Nick'll dry, won't you, Nick?"

"And I'll take a look at the television for you," said Ed Black.

So he's going to make himself useful, thought Nick, as he took the drying-up cloth from its hook. Not that he would be here long enough to be of much use.

"How are the Simpsons?" he asked.

"The Simpsons? Oh, fine."

"The baby'll be walking now, is he?" said Nick, laying a trap, feeling mean, but determined to press on.

"But they don't have a baby. Not the Simpsons I know."

Not the Simpsons that Nick knew either.

After lunch he cycled the eight miles into the hinterland to see Joe. He passed farmhouses built of golden stone and red pantiled roofs, with barns stacked full of gleaming wheat. A low mist hung above the straw-coloured fields. Spears of russet and red flamed against the pale sky. It was quiet inland, away from the sea.

He stopped and for a while watched a lime green tractor ploughing a dark brown field with a cloud of birds following in its wake. He wanted to paint the tractor and the field. He wanted to paint everything he saw every day, even the round face of Mrs Plummer staring from behind its plate glass window. If he painted her he might be able to exorcise her evil power.

Joe lived in the end house of a row of terraced farm cottages. His mother worked for the farmer's wife, his father drove long-distance lorries, as Joe intended to do himself when he was old enough. Juggernauts to Europe: that was his ambition. He loved travelling, on anything, anywhere.

On the piece of ground at the side of the house he was working on his car. He looked up as Nick approached.

"Hi, Rembrandt!" He waved a screwdriver.

"Hi, grease monkey!" Nick parked his bicycle and sat down on an old car seat which Joe had picked up somewhere. The springs had long gone but it was remarkably comfortable. He enjoyed watching Joe work. His fingers were deft and sure and he seemed to know exactly what he was doing. Machines were a mystery to Nick, though they fascinated him.

"How's it going?"

"Okay. Dad brought me back a distributor last night. Bit of luck that! He found it on an old wreck that had been abandoned."

"I don't know why you don't become a mechanic."

"I want to drive, that's why. I'm restless – you know me!" Joe grinned, tightened a nut and sat up straight, pushing his thick brown hair out of his eyes and smearing his face with more grease. "Anyway, I can always be a mechanic later if I change my mind, can't I?"

"Of course. Or you could go to college and get a proper qualification."

"College, me? Don't talk daft! I'll never get enough O grades."

"You could, if you tried."

"I doubt it. Come on in for a cup of tea."

Mr Marks was watching Grandstand on television, Mrs Marks was doing her ironing. Her head was covered with rollers and tied up in a chiffon scarf. Saturday night was their big night out.

"Hello, Nick," she said. "Thought I saw you from the window. How's your mum then? Keeping busy?"

"Yes thanks, very."

"She'll be missing your dad?"

"Yes," said Nick and followed Joe into the small narrow kitchen.

"There's a cup of tea in the pot," Mrs Marks called after them.

There was just room for the two boys to sit at the table.

"You know, Joe, you shouldn't put yourself down. About your school work. You'll get your O grades if you just do a bit of work."

"And Dad doesn't move his job."

"He's not thinking of it, is he?" said Nick, alarmed. Joe had been here for two years and was the best friend he'd ever had.

"I shouldn't think so. He just talks. Likes the idea as much as anything else. But Mum's getting a bit fed up with moving."

Nick sat back relieved. If Mrs Marks was against it, they wouldn't go.

"Hey, is that the time?" Joe caught hold of Nick's wrist and looked at his watch. "I'll need to get myself cleaned up." He went to the sink and, turning on the tap, began washing his hands, arms and face vigorously under the running water.

"Where are *you* going?"

Joe's reply was muffled under the towel. He dried the back of his neck and arms, carefully, not looking at Nick.

"What's going on?" asked Nick, amused.

Joe looked a bit red in the face, though it might only have been from the rubbing of the towel. "I've got a date."

"Oh."

"I'm taking Katy McIlroy to the pictures in Edinburgh. We've got to get the five bus."

"I'll be getting along then." Nick placed his mug on the draining board. "See you Monday."

The light was ebbing as he cycled back towards the sea. The lime green tractor lay idle at the edge of the brown field, the gulls had gone.

As he opened the front door of his house he heard the unmistakable voice of his Belfast grandmother coming from the kitchen.

Chapter Four

Although Mrs McLintock had spent the last forty-five years of her life in Scotland, she still retained the accent of her native city.

"And when am I going to meet him then?" she demanded. She wore her hat and sat so close to the stove that Nick wondered that her knees did not burn. In her hand she held a cup and saucer. Saucers were only brought out when she came on a visit.

"I've told you, Mother —" Mrs Murray was trying not to sound exasperated, "— he doesn't come down except at breakfast. He's not having full board."

"And where does he eat the rest of the time?"

"Chip shop," said Nick.

Mrs McLintock sniffed. "That's not good for anyone. And if he brings the stuff in here he'll smell the place out."

Mrs Murray refilled the cups and cut the chocolate cake. It was thick and moist. Nick took a large slice and ate it hungrily. The cycle run in the sharp air had given him an appetite. He could feel his cheeks tingling.

"So what foot does he kick with then?" asked Mrs McLintock, not allowing herself to be diverted by chocolate cake. She herself kicked with the right, since she was a Protestant. An ardent one, suspicious of the Pope and his wanderings. He was just trying to get more people into his own fold, she maintained, and thereby weaken the Protestants.

"Honestly, Mother!"

"It's a perfectly harmless question, Rona."

"Is it?"

"In what way *is* it harmful then, tell me that?"

"Why ask it? Okay, so I know you can't help it."

"And what's that supposed to mean?"

Nick licked the chocolate off his fingers. They were getting really warmed up now.

"Nothing! I just can't stand the way you want to label people, divide them up."

"It's just so as I can place them."

"Anyway, it doesn't matter what foot he kicks with, Mother. More tea?" Mrs Murray's voice was cool, in contrast to her face, which looked hot.

"Has he any pictures of the Virgin Mary or the like? They're always a dead giveaway."

"They would be wouldn't they?" Her daughter's sarcasm went unregistered. "But I have no intention of going into his room. He's going to do for himself for the short time he's here."

"Oh, I wouldn't allow that!"

There were a lot of things she wouldn't allow, thought Nick, and if she knew what her precious granddaughter was getting up to half the time she'd have a fit. Especially if she knew that Andrea had a Roman Catholic boyfriend.

After she had finished her tea Mrs McLintock went upstairs to the bathroom. She could have used the downstairs toilet but said she preferred the bathroom. She seemed to be away for a long time. Mrs Murray moved restlessly around the kitchen washing up, wiping down the draining board and counters. She went over all of them twice.

"Can't think why she should be *so* bothered about it all," said Nick.

"It's her background, it's about time you understood that. All the men in her family have been Orangemen as far back as anyone can remember." His mother's voice was bitter, surprisingly so really, for he would have thought she would have taken it all as a matter of course by now. After all, they didn't affect her life in any way. She only had her own mother to contend with, and that she was able to do.

"So our ancestors fought at the Boyne? For King Billy?"

"I daresay. And the present lot are still fighting it."

"Hardline, you might call them," said Nick, and drew a straight black line across a piece of white paper.

"You might well."

Mrs McLintock returned, obviously having had no luck with the lodger.

"He seems a quiet fella?"

"He is," said her daughter. "Very quiet."

They heard the front door opening.

"Would that be him now?" Mrs McLintock inclined her head.

But it was Andrea, and her grandmother was pleased to see her. She held her at arm's length and told her how bonny she was growing. "You're prettier every time I see you!" Andrea laughed and kissed her grandmother's cheek under the curve of the felt brim.

"And have you a young man then, Andrea?"

"Carl-o," said Nick, separating the syllables. He avoided the eye of his mother who was doing her best to quell him.

"What did Nick say his name was?"

"Carl," said Andrea, ending the name with a cough and not looking at anyone in particular.

"Is he at the school with you?"

"No, he's not at school."

"He left in the Middle Ages," said Nick.

"Why don't you go and stick your head in the rain bucket?" said Andrea.

Mrs McLintock laughed. She liked a girl to be spirited. "Tell me about him then, dear, Where did you meet him?"

"The corner café."

"The Sea View?" Mrs McLintock didn't like the sound of that.

Mrs Murray gave Nick another warning look. He went up to his room and drew a tractor with a lime green pastel on a sheet of brown sugar paper. Then he took up the white and began on the cloud of seagulls.

"Nick!" his mother called from downstairs. "Granny's going now. Will you walk her to the bus with Andrea?"

They walked one on either side of their grandmother.

"Your mother was looking a bit drawn I thought," she said, taking a firm grip of their arms as they set off. The pavement was icing over. "Of course she hasn't had an easy life."

Her opening remarks, when she got them alone, were always along these lines. Nick and Andrea exchanged a glance over the top of her hat. Their grandmother's criticism forged a bond between them which helped them hold their tongues. There was no point in unleashing them, that they knew well.

"Your father seems to be sticking to this job. Well, so far at any rate. Mind you, with *his* record –"

"It can't be very easy for him working in that terrible heat," said Andrea, butting in, unable to hold her tongue any longer. "Temperatures are well over a hundred in the shade."

Nick supposed that his father would be working in an air-conditioned kitchen; but still, when he put his foot outside it, the heat *would* be terrible. With the cold air nipping his cheeks, he found it difficult to imagine such heat, just as, in summertime, he could not imagine cold.

He was in two minds as to whether he wanted his father to keep the job or not. He hoped that he would so that he would prove to doubters like his grandmother that he could but, on the other hand, he didn't want him to stay away indefinitely. Even to think that he might, caused him a pang.

"A job's a job," said their grandmother. "Especially these days. And your father was never that great at bending his back."

"That's not true!" said Andrea. "He always helped Mum a lot in the house. He did the fires and all the cooking —"

"There's the bus," said Nick.

They stood on the pavement and waved until the lights of the bus faded into the distance.

"I'm fond of her, you know," said Andrea, "but she is a trial! I'm going up to see Mandy. Will you tell Mum? I won't be late."

"Aren't you seeing Carlo tonight?"

36

"They're very busy, they've got a big party coming in. So there wouldn't be much point in me going in just to hang about."

"Couldn't you have made yourself useful? Waited on table or something of the sort?"

"He only has male waiters."

"Talk about discrimination! Wouldn't you call that being a male chauvinist pig? You've got to watch these Italians, you know. Look at Mario — he wants his wife to have ten children! No women's lib for her. Barefoot, pregnant and in the kitchen — that's her lot."

"Not *all* Italians are the same, Smartass! And I could have killed you, by the way, for telling Gran about Carlo."

"I only said his name," said Nick innocently. "What's in a name?" He danced out of her reach. "See you later!"

On his way back he stopped off at the chip shop for a bottle of lemonade. Ed Black was standing at the counter waiting for chicken and chips. He must have come up the street only a few minutes behind them. Nick wondered if he had heard their grandmother's voice and lain low, or been warned to lie low?

"Salt and sauce?" said Toni, salt shaker at the ready.

"Please."

Nick left with the lodger.

"Chip, Nick? Help yourself."

"No thanks, Mr Black. I've just eaten."

"Call me Ed, please."

Mrs Murray was in the hall when they came in. "Fancy a cup of coffee? And a piece of chocolate cake?"

"I'd love some," said Ed.

He enjoyed the coffee and cake, was plied with more. Mrs Murray loved to see people eat well and her son often disappointed her.

"It must be chilly up at the top of the house," she said. "The room's not really suitable for winter visitors."

"It's fine," said Ed. "I've lived in worse."

"I don't suppose you play Scrabble do you? Sometimes Nick and I have a game together."

Ed had never played and didn't think he'd be much good at it, but said he wouldn't mind a game of cards.

"Do we have any cards anywhere, Nick?" asked his mother. They hadn't played for years, except at their grandmother's. She was fond of a game of cards. Nick got up to search and in a drawer in the dining room – which they only used in summer – found an old pack of dog-eared cards. But it was intact.

Ed suggested a game of gin rummy.

"You'll have to instruct us," said Mrs Murray, laughing.

They settled round the table. Ed shuffled and dealt the cards like a man well practised. Nick lifted his cards, eased them into a fan. It was like going back in time, sitting round the table like this, with a fire at their backs, pulling out from the spread of cards the slender Ace of Diamonds, the Jack of Spades – what a sharp looking fellow he was! – and the pretty-faced Queen of Hearts. When his grandmother used to babysit they would play cards and she'd get so involved that she'd let them stay up long past their bedtime.

"The Ace of Clubs!" declared his mother triumphantly, slipping it in front of the King.

"You're a lucky one aren't you?" said Ed.

She smiled, though why she should Nick did not know, for the old saying said, lucky at cards, unlucky at love. It was his grandmother who had taught them that one.

Ed dealt again. They played several games and laughed a lot and drank more coffee and finished up the chocolate cake.

"It was a good evening, wasn't it?" said his mother after the lodger had gone upstairs.

The morning was fine and clear. Nick got up early and walked on the beach.

Someone else had been before him. The footprints were a man's, large, the right foot less cleanly defined than the left. Before he came to the clump of rocks and found Ed sitting in their shelter, he knew that the prints had been made by him.

"It's great to be out in the early morning, isn't it?" said Ed.

"I only get up early on Saturdays and Sundays."

Ed smiled. He sat gazing out to sea. "I could watch it for hours."

"Me too," said Nick, settling on a rock a few yards from him.

There was a strong swell and the waves were coming rolling in, in long straight powerful lines. They watched as each curled and broke at the height of its power and then crashed on to the sand in a raging froth of white. The sound was hypnotic. But the wind was icy and Ed began to cough. He looked unwell, thought Nick.

"Shall we walk along a bit?" said Ed.

They walked close to the waves, turning in towards one another to speak.

"I used to love going to the sea when I was a boy," said Ed. "We only went on day trips, couldn't afford proper holidays. We used to go to the Antrim coast and watch the Atlantic breakers coming in."

"Mum did too when she was young. But she doesn't go back to Northern Ireland now any more, nor does my grandmother. Not since my great-uncle was shot by the IRA."

"That was a bad business."

"She told you?"

"Yes."

Nick decided to be bold. "Were you in a pub or something like that when the bomb went off?"

"No. It was a car bomb. We just happened to be going by. It wasn't meant for us particularly."

"We?"

"My wife and I. She was killed."

A gull wheeled low over their heads. Nick watched it go seawards skimming the crests of the waves. The sound of the sea filled the silence between them. What could he say now? That he was sorry? He was sorry that he had asked the question.

They went as far as the headland and turned. As they came up the steps from the beach to the road Ed said, "I wouldn't mind seeing some of your pictures. Only if you'd like to show them to me of course."

After breakfast Nick took him up to his room. His mother looked pleased to see them going upstairs together. She was always going on at him about spending too much time on his own, but he needed time by himself in order to see things properly. If you were a painter you had to take time to look.

"They're not all that great," he said diffidently as he indicated the stack of paintings standing against the wall.

Squatting, Ed examined each picture carefully, and when he found one that he especially liked he sat back and looked at it for several minutes.

"I like this."

"That's my friend Joe working on an old car."

"There's a lot of life in it."

"There's a lot of life in Joe."

"And that's you watching isn't it?"

Nick looked at himself, tall and dark, looking like a thinner, younger version of his father, at the edge of the picture. Joe filled the middle ground.

"You've caught your own likeness very well."

"Thanks."

Nick brought out water colours and pencil drawings and spread them on the floor, the bed, the table. They pored over them together, Nick talking, telling how he had come to do each one, and what he planned to do in the future.

The morning passed and they were both surprised when Mrs Murray opened the door to announce that lunch was ready. "Would you like to join us, Ed? I've got a big piece of roast pork and Andrea's gone to Edinburgh."

"Are you sure now?"

"Absolutely."

In that case, said Ed, he'd be delighted to accept, especially with that fantastic smell coming up the stairs.

The meat was delicious, the crackling crisp, and Mrs

40

Murray brought out a bottle of cheap red wine to go with it. Outside, a few flakes of snow were whirling about.

Not a bad way to spend Sunday, Nick decided, as he sipped the wine and watched his mother carve the meat. The meal was leisurely, stretched across the waning afternoon and became tea, and after that they began to play cards again and before he knew it the day was gone and he was in bed, watching the snow drift down against the black square of his uncurtained window. He heard the voices of his mother and Ed talking in the kitchen below. He was rather sorry now that the lodger was to leave the next day.

They were still talking when he fell asleep.

Chapter Five

In the morning Ed Black had a raging temperature. After taking one look at him, Mrs Murray ordered him back to bed and phoned the doctor.

"He won't be able to go today," said Andrea.

"I can hardly put him out when he's ill can I?"

"I wasn't suggesting that you should."

Whilst they were at school the doctor came and said that Ed had a bad attack of 'flu and should stay in bed for a few days.

"Mum loves having someone to fuss over," said Andrea. "It'll draw the fire off us."

"Off you, you mean."

"No, you never get up to anything you shouldn't do you?"

Her words stung. Nick filled the kettle noisily, to drown out the rest of her words. When he turned the tap off she was saying something about getting down to work and only going out three nights a week.

"Only three! Sounds like a real sacrifice to me."

The door bell rang and he trudged off to answer it since Andrea showed no sign of moving. Katy McIlroy's red-haired friend was standing on the mat hugging some sheets of music to her chest.

"Oh hello," he said. He had seen her already that day, at the morning interval.

"I've come for my lesson."

"Oh yes, yes of course."

He stepped aside and let her come into the hall. In the music room the current pupil was still playing.

"I think I'm a minute or two early. I'll just wait here." She indicated the upright chair beside the hall table.

It would be cold sitting there but he had no intention of asking her into the kitchen.

"I don't suppose she'll be long," he muttered.

The kitchen door opened a crack and Andrea peered out to see who it was.

"Oh hello, Susan. Come on in and get warm."

Nick followed Susan along the hall into the kitchen. Andrea pulled up another chair in front of the fire and offered a cup of coffee.

"Thanks very much, Andrea, but I don't think I'd have time."

The two girls started talking about fencing. It seemed that Susan belonged to the school club too.

"You should come back, Nick," said Andrea. "You weren't half bad at it."

"Thanks a lot!"

He had been thinking that he might go back but didn't fancy the idea now, not if he was going to encounter the Katy McIlroy trio there. He was getting too much of them as it was. They heard the door of the music room opening. Susan got up.

"Come back and have a coffee when you've finished," said Andrea.

Susan said that she'd love to and went for her lesson.

"She's one of the best of the younger ones," said Andrea.

"At what?"

"Fencing of course! Do you never listen?"

"Not if I can help it."

She said she despaired of him, and picked up a book on quantum physics. Before Susan's lesson finished Nick went up to his room. She was playing the same piece by Mozart that her friend had played. But she wasn't so bad. He stayed in his room until the coast was clear and she had gone.

He saw her the next morning, and the next. He felt frustrated, he would just be getting going on to something interesting with Joe when they would hear the high voice of Katy McIlroy reaching them on the wind. They then continued down the hill as a fivesome and at the shop Joe and Katy took orders and joined the queue leaving him standing outside with the two attendants. Standing like a dummy.

After it had happened three times in a row he told Joe

that he didn't think he'd bother going down the hill that day, he had to finish his Maths homework which was due to be handed in that afternoon.

"Okay," said Joe, not reading anything in to it. "Want me to get you something?"

"No thanks."

Squatting with his back against the bicycle shed wall, Nick finished the piece of homework in five minutes, and went for a walk round the playground. The enclosed rectangle was a whirl of noise and movement. Kids were pushing and shoving, playing chasey, some younger ones skipping. Behind the sheds others were huddled in groups rolling cigarettes and feverishly puffing away. And everybody, whether still or in motion, seemed to be putting something into his or her mouth. Food, drink, or cigarettes. The smokers looked furtive, were watching over their shoulders whilst trying to appear sophisticated at the same time. Difficult to get the two together at once. He would have liked to have had a go at painting all this hectic activity but if he was to set up his easel here he'd probably get it broken over his head. He grinned.

At the gate he paused to survey the scene on the hill. Kids swarmed up and down. Moving slowly, hand in hand, were Joe and Katy McIlroy. He ducked back behind the gatepost. They hadn't seen him.

At school Joe was preoccupied with Miss McIlroy and at home Nick's mother with ministering to the sick. She was up and down the stairs sixty times a day – or so it seemed – bearing medicine, cups of tea, bowls of broth. She wouldn't let Nick or Andrea go into the room, since Ed had a particularly virulent strain of 'flu, and she didn't want either of them to catch it. One patient in the house was enough. Nick went as far as the door and conversed with Ed briefly, just asking how he was and telling him he was better off in bed in this weather. Ed looked and sounded weak. He would never be back on his feet and able to travel by the end of this week.

On Friday evening he came downstairs in his dressing

gown and sat by the stove for a while. They played rummy, but after two games his strength began to flag and Mrs Murray, who had been watching with concern, packed him off to bed again.

"Can I get you anything in Edinburgh?" asked Nick. "I'm going in the morning."

But there was nothing that Ed seemed to want.

Nick took an early bus into Edinburgh. Frost sparkled on the fields, the day promised to be bright and clear. He enjoyed the ride.

Edinburgh looked good too, under a winter blue sky with the rooftops and spires standing starkly black against it. He walked through Princes Street gardens, watched a man feeding pigeons and went up the Mound to buy paints to replenish his stocks, as well as some soft black pencils. He idled in the shop buying more than he really needed and left himself with only ten pence in his pocket and his return ticket.

Grandmother McLintock was next on the list. His mother had given him a cake to take to her. He knew it was only an excuse to get him to go there. "She loves getting visits from you and Andrea," she had said, placing the cake in a tin and the tin in his rucksack. And Granny wasn't getting any younger. And she didn't see that many people. And he was her only grandson. He knew all the reasons that he should go. The funny thing was that although he made a fuss, once he was there he didn't mind, even quite enjoyed himself.

She lived in a tenement flat on the other side of the Meadows, a big sweep of green crisscrossed with paths and lined with trees that separated the old town from the beginnings of the suburbs. He joined the stream of people moving up Middle Meadow Walk.

His grandmother was at home and pleased to see him, as his mother had predicted. She sat him down and had the kettle on and the small table set in front of the fire almost before he could get his breath back from running up the three flights of stairs. He sat down and relaxed, as she told him to do. Her flat had a strange hypnotic effect on him. The fire was heaped high and roaring half way up the chimney as if it wanted to escape, the room was crowded with knick-knacks which he would have hated to live with but liked in his grandmother's house. Souvenirs from Bangor, Portrush and Donaghadee – all places in Northern Ireland – stood on the mantelpiece and mahogany sideboard beside china shepherdesses and framed portraits of her family. There stood his great-grandfather the Worshipful Grand Master wearing his orange sash and medallions from the First World War. And there his two great-uncles, one now dead from an IRA bullet.

"Fresh baked this morning," said his grandmother, laying a plate of fruit scones on the table. "I must have known you were coming."

It was impossible to refuse her food. He took a scone (still warm) and spread it with butter and drank the thick, dark tea which she had brewed. You could have stood on her tea if you'd been of a mind to.

She pulled up her chair at the other side of the fire.

"Give us all your crack then, Nick. Have you still that lodger with you?"

Nick gave her an up-to-date report on Ed and his illness. His grandmother thought his mother had enough to do without having to look after a sick man. "She doesn't seem to mind," said Nick. In fact, she likes it, he thought; she was cheerful and her step on the stair was light.

"Do you know anything more about him then? His background and that?"

"Not much." Nick finished his scone and was immediately offered another which he took. "Why do you hate Catholics, Gran?"

"But I don't hate them, lad." She was shocked. "I may not agree with them but I don't hate them. It's just that I think they're misguided, poor souls. Worshipping graven images and burning incense and confessing their sins through a grille." She shuddered. She had never been in a

Catholic church, though could well imagine it.

"Gran, what happened to your brother George?"

Mrs McLintock frowned. "Why you know what happened to him, Nick. He was shot by an IRA gunman."

"But why?"

"For no good reason, son, no good reason!" Her cheeks blazed like the fire at their feet. "He wouldn't have hurt a fly, so he wouldn't. He was a good Protestant: that was all they had against him."

She is lying, he thought; there was more to it than that. He could tell by her eyes that what she told was not the whole truth.

"Did they get the gunman?"

"Oh yes they got his all right! Michael Doyle." Mrs McLintock dwelt on the name for a moment. "And another UDR man was killed in front of his children just yesterday. What kind of a beast would do a thing like that, would you tell me? Is there never going to be any end to it?"

It seemed not. A bomb had gone off in a Catholic pub last night: they had heard it on the news that morning. Ed Black had shaken his head but said nothing. An eye for an eye . . . Nick sighed. All over the world people continued to take an eye for an eye and a tooth for a tooth. What a terrible waste of life and time it was when there were so many good things they could be doing! Like building a new car from the wreck of an old one, or painting pictures. His grandmother was staring into the flames. He wished he could see what she saw.

"Gran, could I come and paint you one day?"

"Paint me? Whatever would you want to do that for?" But she was pleased, her face flushed, and she smiled. If he was really sure he wanted to then she wouldn't object.

"Thank you." He stretched. He must be going, he had other things to do.

"And what about your lunch?"

"I never eat much in the middle of the day."

That was a mistake. She gave him a lecture on the perils of not eating enough to keep your strength up, put an apple in his rucksack for him to eat on the bus and told him to come back soon. He ran down the three flights of stairs out into the fresh morning. It was funny how he hated her prejudices and yet was fond of her. Of course she was his own flesh and blood. Not that that always meant much. His mother had hated her Uncle George.

On the bus he thought about Uncle George and his mother and Ed Black. There was something about the lodger that still troubled him.

On the doorstep of the house he met Ed, wrapped in a woollen scarf and an old heavy coat of Mr Murray's which he had been told to make use of.

"I'm just going to walk along the headland. I couldn't stand being boxed up inside any longer."

Nick nodded. He could understand that feeling.

He closed the front door. His mother's pupil was playing chords and his mother was talking. The rest of the house was quiet. Andrea would be with Carlo.

Nick raced up the stairs taking three steps at a time. He knew what he was going to do, he had been thinking about it all week and had argued with himself back and forth about the rights and wrongs of it. He had decided that at the first opportunity he was going to take a look at Ed Black's room.

In all sorts of places people were doing the most extraordinary things nowadays. In hotel rooms and boarding houses they made bombs which sometimes went off accidentally. You read about it in the papers. How was he to know if Ed Black had been telling the truth about a car bomb going off as he happened to be passing? And how would you recognise a terrorist if you met one?

He opened the door of the lodger's room and went inside, leaving the door open so that he could listen for sounds below.

He did a quick survey of the room. On the bedside table there were half a dozen paperbacks (his mother's), an old radio (theirs), a couple of car magazines and today's *Scotsman*; on the floor their portable television set taken apart with the pieces arranged in neat and tidy fashion. He opened the wardrobe: from the rail hung one pair of trousers and three shirts, on the floor sat a pair of black shoes. The door squeaked as he closed it. His heart was beating very fast and very loud. His hands were sweating. He felt like a thief. He went to the window and looked along the beach. He saw Ed walking towards the headland, a tall, slightly stooped figure moving slowly.

Only two drawers of the chest were in use. They held underwear, socks, washbag, writing paper and envelopes. He replaced them carefully. Under the bed he found a pair of slippers and the holdall and suitcase he had arrived with. Pulling them out Nick saw he had disturbed the dust. But he couldn't bother about that now. In the holdall there was dirty washing, and in the suitcase nothing at all. Though, just a minute, there *was* something in the side pocket.

The doorbell rang downstairs. It would not be Ed: he had been given a key. Nick checked from the window: jumble sale collectors.

Out of the suitcase pocket he took an old leather wallet – and a rosary. So Ed was a Catholic! Why should that matter? Only because his grandmother made such an issue of it. If it weren't for her he wouldn't even have thought about it. The doorbell rang again.

"Nick!" his mother was calling. He stayed still. He heard her go to open the door.

He opened the wallet. In it were three photographs, one much older than the other two. They were photographs of three women, one elderly, one middle-aged, one young.

The elderly woman looked like Ed's mother and the middle-aged one like his wife. And the young one? Nick frowned. This was the old photograph; it was a little faded and cracked, but the girl's face was still fresh and clear. She was laughing and she had long blonde hair blowing around her shoulders. Surely it couldn't be . . . But it could. It was.

It was a picture of his mother taken when she was young.

Chapter Six

He had to talk to someone. It was out of the question to tell Andrea who would go straight to their mother and confront her with it. There was only one person he could tell whom he could trust.

Cycling out to Joe's he did not notice the brown fields, the lime green tractor, the following gulls; he saw only the laughing face of his mother as she had been at eighteen or nineteen. She had been the image of what Andrea was now.

His mother had lied to them too. Why had she not just said, "This is Ed Black, an old friend of mine. We used to know one another when we were young."

The assortment of machinery beside the Marks's house lay idle. No one sat on the old car seat. Nick dismounted and rang the bell.

Mrs Marks came to the door with her head done up in the usual rollers and scarf.

"Oh hello, Nick. Looking for Joe, are you? He went out an hour ago. I thought he might have been going to see you?" Nick shook his head. They exchanged a few remarks on the state of the weather and then Mr Marks called out, "There's a terrible draught, Phyll. It's turning the place into a fridge. Bring the lad in, don't keep him on the doorstep!"

Nick picked up his bicycle, refusing cups of tea and a heat up at the fire. "Are you sure now, lad?" said Mrs Marks. "Sure", he said.

He rode home slowly. At a set of crossroads he hesitated, and took the right hand turn, not the left which was more direct.

This road went past Katy McIlroy's house. Her father was tractorman on a farm along here, her family lived in one of the farm cottages.

The cottages were set close to the road. As he approached them he saw Joe's scarlet and white bike leaning against the gable end wall. Accelerating, he swept past, head bent low over the handlebars.

And when he saw Joe on Monday morning he knew that he couldn't tell him about Ed Black and his mother's photograph after all for he realised that Joe might well be embarrassed by the confidence and would probably only say something like it was best to let sleeping dogs lie. Joe had told him once that he believed in letting the past *be* past. Nick had been asking him about the places he used to live in. "When you've got to move on, Rembrandt, then you've just got to go and there's no point looking over your shoulder." That was how he had put it.

Nick let himself be persuaded to go down to the shop that morning. "You can't have homework to finish off every day," said Joe.

The girls were talking excitedly about a party Katy was planning to have at her house on Saturday night. Her parents were going away for the week-end.

"Are they leaving you on your own?" asked Nick. Whenever his mother went away – which was seldom – they had awful rows about not being allowed to stay on their own. Andrea was always furious, claiming that her mother didn't trust her, and as for having their grandmother to stay, it was more a case of *them* looking after *her* rather than the other way round.

"My older sister'll be there."

"She's nineteen," said the fair-haired girl whose name he had gathered to be Jane. Her father was the farmer who employed Mr McIlroy.

"You'll come, won't you, Nick?" said Katy.

"Me? Oh no thanks, parties aren't in my line."

"Come on, Rembrandt, give it a try!" said Joe.

But Nick shook his head and would not be persuaded. To stop the clamour he asked them what they wanted and joined the queue himself.

"I'll give you a hand," said Susan.

"It's okay, I can manage."

That seemed to annoy her. Whisking round on her heel, she went back to join Jane. She didn't speak to him on the way back up the hill. That suited him well enough.

Anyway, the only topic of conversation they had was who was to be asked to the party. It sounded like half the school would be going. How they would cram them all into that small cottage was beyond him.

"Not very sociable, are you?" said Joe at Geography afterwards.

"No. But I don't have to be, do I?"

"Guess not."

"But you are?"

"I like a good party," said Joe with a grin.

"Want to come home at lunchtime? Mum's got the soup pot on."

"That'd have been great, Nick, but I've said I'd go to the Sea View with Katy."

"Enough talking at the back," said the Geography teacher.

When Nick got home he found Ed sitting at the kitchen table in his dressing gown and Mrs Murray serving the soup. Cream of celery. They had a different kind every day now.

"You've gone on a real soup bender," said Nick.

"Yes, I have, haven't I?" said his mother absent-mindedly. Sometimes he had the feeling that she didn't quite hear what he said these days.

"This is fantastic," said Ed after the first spoonful, almost before it had time to touch down. Mrs Murray glanced up and her eyes met his and they smiled. Nick looked back down at his plate. He wasn't as hungry as he'd thought.

"There's a letter from Dad, by the way," said his mother. Did she sound off-hand about it or was he beginning to imagine things? He got up and fetched the letter from where she had propped it behind the toast rack.

His father was good at writing letters. He wrote as he talked, informally, telling stories. He wrote about the job and the other men, particularly the men, bringing them to life. Nick smiled as he read. Whenever a letter came it partly brought his father back to him.

"Dad seems to be having a good time in spite of everything." In spite of the heat and being away from home.

"Yes, he does, doesn't he? Your father always would of course, no matter where he went."

"What's wrong with that?"

"I never said there was anything wrong with it. Aren't you going to finish your soup?"

"Sorry. But I'm not hungry."

She didn't even sigh, the way she would have done before Ed Black had come on the scene, their scene.

He pulled on his anorak. "I'm off."

"Cheerio," said Ed. "See you later."

Nick heard them laughing as he left the house. It was far too early to go back to school.

As he was passing the café Joe rapped on the window and waved him in. Mrs Plummer and Mrs Ramage were sitting in their usual places.

"I hear your lodger's ill?" said Mrs Plummer, who seldom addressed him.

"Yes, he's had 'flu."

"That'll be a lot of extra work for your mother?" said Mrs Ramage. "I imagine she's got enough to do without that."

"He's getting better now though." Nick moved on to Joe and Katy's table. Jane was there too, drinking Coca Cola.

"Funny if you ask me," he heard Mrs Ramage say in her not-so-soft voice. The two heads moved in towards one another over the table and the chins started to wag. And every now and then they glanced over their shoulders at him. Mrs Ramage would blot her ruby red lips with her paper serviette before opening them to make her next pronouncement. They were talking about his mother and the lodger, he knew that. *And with Mr Murray away too . . .*

"What are you having then, Nick?" asked Mario.

"Yes, wake up, Rembrandt!" said Joe.

"Coffee please, Mario."

Before long Susan came in, and they were off again about the party. Katy was writing names on the inside back page of her homework notebook. Nick was glad when it was time to shift up the hill.

"I never see you now without all these women around," he complained in the cloakroom which was mercifully confined to boys.

Joe laughed. "Come on home with me after school."

Mrs Marks insisted that Nick stay to tea. He rang home to tell his mother. "That's very nice, dear. I'm sure you'll have a good evening with Joe. He's such a nice boy." Usually she would be fussing about him riding back in the dark and asking if his lights were all right. "Take care," she said before she rang off, as a kind of afterthought. Her thoughts were obviously elsewhere.

Mr Marks had set off that morning for France and would be away all week.

"It doesn't worry me now," said Mrs Marks. "I'm used to it. He's usually home of a week-end which is the main thing. It won't be so easy for your mother. Your father'll only be home a couple of times a year, won't he?"

"I suppose so."

"I've got a nice piece of fish for you," she said, setting it in front of them, "and a few chips." The few chips turned out to be more like a mountain. She was going next door to have a bite with her neighbour who lived alone. "She likes a bit of company. Everybody does, don't they?" Before she went she put a bottle of cider on the table. "Enjoy yourselves!"

And they did. Nick ate half the chips and drank his share of the cider. They sat at the fire finishing the bottle off. His appetite was always bigger in the Marks's house. Mrs Marks thought men should eat like horses and would have been astounded if you left anything on your plate.

"I wish I was on my way to France," said Joe.

"Same here!"

"When I've got my car on the road we'll go travelling in Europe. I'll drive and you can bring your painting gear along. You could paint portraits and I'll collect the money in a hat. How about it?"

"You're on! I wish we could leave tomorrow."

"So do I. Then we wouldn't have all these old exams to bother about."

There were things other than exams that Nick would be happy to leave behind. But he didn't mention them.

They sat and talked about travelling and Joe's car and then they had a few games of darts. Nick beat Joe.

"You've got a straight eye, haven't you, Rembrandt? And a straight hand."

"I'd better be going." Nick yawned. "Say thanks to your mother for me will you?"

The night air was bracing after the heat in the Marks's sitting room and woke him up thoroughly. The sky was sprinkled with stars. By the time he'd gone a mile or so he felt he could have cycled all the way to France.

The front of his house was dark. He put away his bicycle and opened the back door.

His mother and Ed were sitting at the table close together. Her hand lay on top of the table and his hand rested over hers, the fingers curling round it.

Chapter Seven

"What made you change your mind then?" asked Joe.

"Well, you *have* been going on at me . . . "

"Wore you down eh! Katy'll be pleased."

Nick knew quite well why he had changed his mind about going to the party and it had nothing to do with the Katy McIlroy trio going on at him. There were two reasons in fact. One was coming home and finding his mother and Ed Black sitting together at the kitchen table. That had left him feeling restless and with the need to do something to let off steam. He hadn't been able to let any off when he did walk into the kitchen. Ed had taken his hand away immediately and his mother had jumped up to ask Nick if he'd had a good time and would he like a cup of hot chocolate? Both she and Ed had carried on as if nothing untoward had happened and, afterwards, lying in bed, Nick wondered if he could have imagined those hands linked together.

He drew the hands now, on the rough book which he kept in his desk and which was full of sketches and squiggles and doodles. Joe craned his neck. "What are you drawing?"

"Hands. They tell you a lot about people."

Joe spread out his own. They were broad, strong hands stained with oil that wouldn't easily wash out, and the nails were chipped.

"See what I mean?" said Nick.

The other reason he had decided to go to the party was Andrea. The words she had flung at him had stayed with him. *You never do anything you shouldn't, do you?* She thought she was such a woman of the world, living dangerously, driving around in a fast red sports car, puffing away on foul-smelling cigarettes, drinking rum and Coke in the chrome-plate cocktail bar of Carlo's restaurant. And then there was Carlo himself, of the shining smile and smooth tongue.

"You've never given Carlo a chance," Andrea had

accused him. "You or Mother. Just because he doesn't paint pictures or play the piano you've no time for him. You're so – narrow-minded!"

"Joe doesn't paint pictures or play the piano and I've got plenty of time for him," he had retaliated.

Narrow-minded indeed! The accusation had made him grind his teeth.

Mrs Murray had come in at the tail-end of the argument and cut it off, telling them it was time they grew up and stopped arguing. "At what age do you think you will stop?"

"When we're in our bath chairs."

"I wouldn't count on that," Andrea had said and grinned at the image of them in wheelchairs hurling insults at one another across the room. And he had grinned too.

"I'm glad you'll be staying at Joe's," said Mrs Murray. She was ironing, a job she hated and did only when she had company in the kitchen. Nick was painting. "I don't like the idea of you coming home late at night on your own, even though you'll be on your bicycle."

"I hardly think I'll be alone. There's a cast of thousands going."

"Still, you can rely on Joe."

Mrs Murray went into the scullery.

She was almost too keen on the idea of him staying at Joe's for the night. Andrea would be in Edinburgh which meant that she and Ed would be in the house on their own. He was uneasy about that but what could he do? Call up his grandmother and ask her to come over and babysit? The idea amused him.

His mother came back with her arms full of damp sheets.

In the hall Andrea was talking on the telephone. She had been there for half an hour.

"I wish I could, Carlo," Nick heard her say. "I'd love to but I can't. I've got a history essay to finish."

She came into the kitchen saying she was fed up, she wished she was thirty and would never have to do another exam as long as she lived. She stood in front of the stove warming her blue hands.

"It's difficult I know, dear," said her mother, intent on trying to fold a sheet.

"Sometimes I wonder if it's worth all the effort."

"Of course it is!"

"It's not as if there'll be any jobs at the end of it."

"There are bound to be some. And it's better to be educated anyway."

Nick leaned forward, frowning with concentration, his brush loaded with dark red paint. He had heard all these arguments before; they all had, in school and out. He considered himself fortunate that he didn't have to think in terms of jobs. That's all very well, his mother would say, but you've got to live. He'd manage somehow, do odd jobs, and if there weren't any then he'd just have to live on the dole until the day came when he sold his paintings for money, real money.

"What are you painting, Nick?" Mrs Murray came to look. "The Sea View Watchers!"

He had painted them seated at their favourite table in the café: Mrs Plummer, moon-faced, plump white hands holding a cup of coffee between them; Mrs Ramage, ruby red lips puckered round a smouldering cigarette, eyes narrowed to slits above the smoke. Between them on the table lay an empty plate.

"It's very good," said Mrs Murray, laughing.

Andrea joined her mother behind Nick's shoulder. "Hey, you've caught them to a t! You've got all the little details right."

"It's not too bad," said Nick off-handedly, hiding his pleasure. It was not often that Andrea really *looked* at his painting and less often that she praised it.

"They look conspiratorial. What's the empty plate for, Nick?"

"Mario's cherry cake. Hadn't got that far yet."

"Looks more suited to somebody's head. You know that picture in the gallery of Salome carrying John the Baptist's head?"

"Ghoulish girl," said Mrs Murray and went to pour a cup of coffee from the pot on the stove. "I'll just take this up to Ed."

"She's very attentive to her patient I must say," said Andrea, when their mother had gone.

The remark was a leading one but Nick did not take it up. He did not want to have Andrea voice what he suspected. With a bit of luck Ed Black would go away in a day or two and they could forget him. He went back to his picture.

"Don't you think so?"

"Mm," he said.

"That's right, go on, bury your head in the sand!"

He darkened Mrs Ramage's underlip and pursed his own lips. Was it as full as that? He thought so. But he must look again the next time he saw her in the café. He saw both women so often that their features were imprinted on his mind.

They seemed to be forever talking about Ed. *Mrs Murray's lodger*. The words buzzed in his ears. When he was with Joe and the girls in the Sea View he wondered that they did not hear them too, but they appeared not to and carried on talking about the party.

Saturday – the big day – arrived. As the morning wore on Nick toyed with excuses not to go. A sore throat. A pain in his stomach. He did actually have a bit of a pain in his stomach but it was coming and going and not seriously troublesome.

Joe rang in the afternoon. "You're not going to change your mind now are you, Rembrandt? I'm just ringing to make sure."

"You'll enjoy yourself once you're there," said his mother, who herself disliked parties and only went to keep his father company.

"Do you like parties, Ed?" asked Andrea.

"Not very much these days. I like to take my pleasures with smaller numbers. But, still, you're young, the two of you, that makes a difference."

Nick felt as old as the hills as he got dressed to go. He put his pyjamas and a bottle of cider into his rucksack, and a box of chocolates which his mother had bought for him to give to Mrs Marks.

"Have a good time!" said Andrea. She was waiting for Carlo to pick her up. "And don't do anything I wouldn't do."

All three members of the Marks's household were looking quite unlike their everyday selves. Mr Marks wore a brown and white striped suit and his wife a shiny black dress with a diamante clip at the neck (they were going to a dinner dance at a roadhouse) and Joe was so clean and slicked down as to be almost unrecognisable. Even the stains had been scrubbed off his hands.

"I wish we were going to stay in and have a game of darts," said Nick gloomily. Joe laughed. "And don't tell me I'll enjoy myself once I get there!"

They went early as Joe had promised to give Katy a hand. When they arrived only Katy and her sister Helen were there, and Jane, since she lived nearby. Sandwiches, bowls of crisps and nuts, stood on the sideboard, and a few bottles of cider. The guests would bring more bottles. Katy was rushing about on high red heels, teetering from kitchen to sitting room to the front door step to survey the road.

"It'll be all right," said Joe, catching hold of her hand. "Don't worry yourself! Let's have a drink."

Nick drank down a tumblerful of cider rather fast, and then another.

"Like a sandwich?" Jane offered a plate of egg and tomato but the sight of food made him feel a bit sick. "I made them myself." He told her he'd just eaten.

Susan came next, dropped off by her father in his car, and then gradually, the others arrived, in twos and threes and fours. The small cottage room rapidly filled up until it was standing room only and not much space to move between the bodies. Music was played non-stop and loudly on the record player. Some attempted to dance but it wasn't easy and drinks got slopped around and shins kicked and feet trodden on. The kitchen filled up too, and the hall, and people sat on the beds in the girls' bedroom. It was a wonder the roof didn't lift off, thought Nick, the way the rooms were vibrating below it. He could imagine the roof rising, taking off into space, and them left gazing up into the night sky.

"Have some wine," said someone, pouring a stream of red liquid into his glass.

Jane, at his elbow, giggled and said she'd drunk two glasses of wine and it was going to her head. Nick felt nothing. At this rate he wouldn't be letting off any steam at all. Perhaps he was gathering it inside him and at a certain point he would explode and let it all come out, in the middle of this wriggling, jiggling fray.

"What's the joke?" asked Jane.

"Nothing."

"Why do you never tell what you're thinking?" The wine had given her courage.

"Because he likes to be secretive," said Susan, ducking under someone's arm to join them.

Secretive? Perhaps he did. Or just was by nature. Maybe you couldn't choose. But he had one great big secret locked inside him.

A boy pushing past jogged Nick's elbow and wine shot out of his glass over his hand. He licked it clean and thought that maybe after all his head did feel just a little affected. He drained his glass. He wanted to be reckless. If he drank enough surely recklessness would come?

"Hold up your glass," shouted Joe. Nick did as he was told and Joe filled the glass with white wine.

"My dad says you should never mix white with red," said Susan.

"My dad said I wasn't to drink anything stronger than Coke," giggled Jane.

"Hope he doesn't come over," said Susan.

"I hope not either!"

"Let's go into the kitchen," said Susan. "They've got hot sausage rolls there. And I wouldn't mind a cup of coffee."

61

"How'll we get through?" said Jane.

"Leave that to me!" said Nick. "I'll lead the way. I'll open up a passage for you like Moses dividing the Red Sea." I must be getting drunk, he thought.

They managed to reach the kitchen which was not so jammed up as the sitting room. Helen was sitting on the draining board dispensing coffee.

"Not for me thanks," said Nick. He held up his glass. "I'll stick to this."

"Want a joint?" asked Jake, a boy in his class.

"Joint?"

"Grass!"

"Oh, of course. Sure."

Jane giggled and spilt her coffee down the front of her blouse. With great deliberation Nick put the limp looking cigarette into his mouth and bent his head to get a light. It went out after the first puff and he had to get it lit again.

"What's it like?" asked Susan.

"Great," he said, though he wasn't sure what anything was like any more. "Want to try?"

"I'm chicken."

"I'll try," said Jane.

"Just you lay off, Jane Bell," said Helen, "or your father'll be after me. You kids shouldn't be smoking that stuff."

But she didn't make any effort to stop them. She would have a job if she tried, thought Nick. Anyone would have a job stopping anything in a mob like this. One or two kids were getting a bit wild, jumping about; one was making a scene about drinking beer out of a can, tipping his head back to let the beer run in a stream down into his mouth. He was half choking and there was beer on his clothes and all over Mrs McIlroy's kitchen floor.

"Hey, give over!" said Helen sharply.

Everything is getting out of hand, thought Nick; *I* am getting out of hand. He felt decidedly strange, as if he wasn't quite all there. He parked his glass on the counter.

The cigarette had gone dead on him again.

"You all right?" said Susan.

"Fine, fine."

"Have a sausage roll."

He shuddered. He had his arm round someone's shoulder, he discovered; he was leaning on it. Was it Jane's or was it Susan's? He could not decide. Both, perhaps.

"Think I'll just go to the loo," he muttered.

It was a fight to get there and there was someone in when he did. He waited, his head back against the wall. Beside him a boy and girl clung to one another as if they were drowning. The beat of the music pulsed through his head. Sweat was breaking out on his forehead like beads of dew.

The bathroom door opened and someone came out. He went in. The walls were tilting away from him, falling outwards, his head was spinning, the white bath was coming up to meet him. He clutched at the rim of the washhand basin with both hands. *Keep your head, hold on, don't let go, breathe deeply, you'll be all right in a minute! Don't let go! Don't.*

As soon as he could risk lifting one hand he turned on the cold tap and sluiced water over his face, again and again and again until he was gasping and the polo neck of his sweater was soaked. He felt a little better, though not much. He must get some air.

As he came out of the bathroom a load of new arrivals drew up in a car outside. The front door was standing open.

"I didn't ask them," Katy was saying. "I've never seen them before."

"Gatecrashers!" said Joe. "I'll deal with them."

Nick moved slowly but purposefully along the narrow hall, unable to deal with anything other than reaching that cool fresh air ahead. "Excuse me!" He might as well talk to himself. He trampled on feet, coats that had fallen off hooks; his toe stubbed against beer cans and empty bottles. The noise on every side was tremendous. Through it he thought he could hear someone call his name but he could not stop.

At last, he felt the air on his face! He stumbled down the one step on to the path and all but fell. Steady now, careful, one step at a time! Joe and a couple of others were arguing with a number of boys who had emerged from both sides of the car. Nick staggered round the side of the house.

Suddenly, he was violently and disgustingly sick. He had never been so sick in his life before. He felt as if he was turned inside out.

When the convulsions had died down, he sat on the ground with his back against the cottage wall. He looked at the stars spread across the wide sky. He could hear a great commotion going on round the corner but it might as well have been a hundred miles away so remote did it seem. He was trembling from head to toe. There was only one thing he wanted to do now: go home to his own bed.

Unsteadily, he got to his feet and made for the back fence. He went over the top in a clumsy forward roll and landed on his back in the ditch. He picked himself up and tried to steer as straight a course as he could down the middle of the road. His head was reasonably clear now so he knew that his limbs were not behaving as he wanted them to. He felt like a rag doll flopping about.

Lights flickering ahead lighting up the trunks of the thin trees warned him that a car was coming. He dived into the ditch just in time. Shaken, he continued, keeping closer to the edge of the road. Just keep going, he told himself, and you'll get there eventually. Each step he took was one step closer to home. Each step was an effort and every so often he had to stop and rest, taking deep gulps of air.

The road was a quiet one with little traffic: only one other car passed him. And the night was quiet too. He had left the noise of the party well behind him. He watched far over to his right the steady wink of the lighthouse.

And there coming up were the lights of the town below! He broke into a run which he could not maintain. He was exhausted. Not far now, you can't give up now! He urged himself on. The lights came closer and closer until he reached the first street lamp. He put his arms round the standard and leaned his forehead against it. He heard a church clock strike one.

Off he went again, trying not to stagger. He passed Mrs Ramage's house. It was dark, thank goodness, though who knew but that she might be watching from behind the curtains even at this late hour? He turned into the High Street. Almost home.

The shops were shuttered and dark. There were a few lights in the flats above them but all had their curtains drawn tight. He could hear the sea now, the soft swish of the waves as they broke on the shore. He rounded the corner into Sea View Terrace. Mrs Plummer had gone to bed too.

For a moment he thought he couldn't find his key and would have to ring the bell. But no, here it was in the back pocket of his jeans. For the first time he realised that he had walked home without his anorak. No wonder he was trembling.

Music was coming from his mother's room above. He was too tired to know what it was. Using the banisters, he hauled himself up the stairs and pushed open the door of her room.

His mother was sitting on the settee with Ed Black. He had his arm round her and her head was resting against his shoulder. Her hair had been loosed from its knot and was floating free. She looked no older than Andrea. She looked as she had done in the photograph in Ed's suitcase.

Chapter Eight

Nick lay in bed unable to sleep in spite of the immense fatigue which swamped him. He could not remember ever having felt so tired, or so ill. Every time he closed his eyes the room rotated. He had to keep them open and the light on. And the pain in his stomach had returned to plague him.

"Try to sleep," his mother had said when she helped him into bed. She had been appalled at the state he was in. Nick had heard Ed saying something in the background about it happening to us all at some time or other and he'd feel better in the morning. Nick doubted if he would feel better, ever.

His mother had cleaned his face with a damp cloth and brought water for him to drink. After a sip his stomach had risen in rebellion again.

"Now you mustn't get the wrong idea about Ed and me," his mother had said, sitting down on the edge of the bed. What idea did she think he had?

He hadn't the strength to ask, to get involved in any kind of discussion, could only say weakly, "Leave me alone please! I don't want to hear about you and him."

He could hear their voices now, murmuring on the other side of the wall. He turned on the radio.

The local station was having a phone-in programme.

"And now we have Elaine on line four. Hello, Elaine. How are you this Sunday morning?" The voice was gentle and sympathetic, one that invited confidences. You could talk to a voice like that, and Elaine was going to.

"Not so good," she said, her voice trembling.

"Why is that, Elaine?"

"I've got this problem."

"Would you like to tell us about it?"

"Well you see I live alone with my dad —"

"Your mother's dead?"

"No. She went away with this other man."

"I see. What age are you, Elaine?"

"Fifteen." Same as he was.

"And how do you get on with your dad?"

"All right, on the whole. Well during the day when he's sober. But at night —"

"He takes a drink?"

"Yes. And when he comes in with a skinful in him —" Elaine faltered. The world waited. Nick waited.

"He's difficult is he, Elaine?" The gentle voice coaxed.

"He beats me up." There: it was out!

There was nothing that you could not confess to. The counsellor began counselling, knowing what to say and saying it with utmost reason. Elaine's problem was not unusual and nothing for her to feel ashamed about; and something could be done about it.

I could phone in, thought Nick; I could go to the call box at the end of the promenade and phone without them hearing me.

'Now we go to line three. We have Nick on line three. Are you there, Nick?'

'Yes, I am here.'

'And how are you this morning?'

'Not so good.' Terrible, if you really want to know. I think I may even be dying.

'Can you tell us about your problem?'

'My father's working abroad and my mother —'

'What about your mother?'

'Well there's this man who's turned up out of the blue. He was in a bomb blast, he might even be a terrorist.'

'A terrorist? What makes you say that?'

'He's from Belfast.'

'Not everyone from Belfast is a terrorist, Nick!' Ha, Ha, what a silly idea!

'I know that. But my mother's uncle was shot by the IRA. On his own doorstep. And she knew this man before he came here. He has her picture —'

'You sound confused, Nick.' Delirous might be a better word. The raging fires of hell could be nothing to the heat in his body. *'You're upset about this man and your mother, aren't you?'*

'*Maybe I am.*' Who wouldn't be? '*She might go away with him, you see.*'

'*Is there anyone you could talk to?*'

'*My grandmother.*'

'*Do you have a good relationship with her?*'

'*All right, I suppose. Though she likes my sister better than me. But she knows all about terrorists.*'

The pain in his stomach doubled him in two. He screamed.

"What day is it?" he asked.

"Monday," said the nurse.

"What happened to Sunday?"

"You slept most of it," she said and popped the thermometer under his tongue.

There were two other beds in the room. In one a young man in green and white striped pyjamas was sitting up reading a magazine, in the other a man with white hair lay flat and sleeping. The outside ledges of the window were white.

"It's been snowing," said the nurse, taking the thermometer out and twisting it sideways to read the numbers. Then she shook the mercury back down.

"Is it bad?"

"It's been worse." She recorded it on the chart at the end of his bed. "You were lucky."

"Was I? You mean I might have been a gonner?"

"Another half hour and you'd have been in a terrible mess. Talk about an erupting appendix!"

"It felt like Mount Vesuvius going off."

She smiled, tucked in the edge of the red blanket, smoothed the sheet under his arms. "You're over the worst now anyway. Your mother'll be in this afternoon. She rang this morning to ask how you were."

She went to attend to the man in the striped pyjamas. "Well, John, and how have you been behaving yourself . . ?"

Nick closed his eyes again. He had no clear recollection

68

of the sequence of events of the last twenty-four – more
than twenty-four – hours. He remembered voices and faces
– his mother's, Ed's, the doctor's – and the agonising ride
into Edinburgh in the ambulance. "Just hang on, lad,
you're going to be all right." He remembered that voice.
Ed's. He remembered the strong feel of the fingers clasping
his wrist. And then the hospital corridors and people in
white and rubber aprons and masks and then . . . Blissful
darkness and silence. Nothing, nothing . . . Until afterwards, wakening fitfully, for brief moments to see dim
lights and blue and white nurses, and back once more into
oblivion.

His side still hurt, but differently, and the room was
steady.

So he'd been drunk and had had a major operation in the
same day! Two firsts. How was that for living dangerously?
It was a lot dicier than being driven by Carlo and drinking
rum and Coke.

His mother came alone that afternoon.

"You gave us an awful shock, you know, Nick."

"Sorry."

"Don't be silly. I'm just so relieved –"

"Ed came with me in the ambulance didn't he?"

"Yes. He was very calm, that's why he went with you.
I thought I might just agitate you so I followed behind in
the car. It was Ed who first suspected appendicitis. He
phoned for the doctor and for the ambulance too, without
waiting for the doctor to come."

"Perhaps he saved my life?"

"Not quite. The surgeon did that. But I don't know what
I'd have done without him. Nick –" She hesitated and then
went on in a rush, "Nick, about that night –"

"It doesn't matter, Mum, really it doesn't. You don't
have to say anything."

"But, Nick –"

He closed his eyes, closed her out. So his illness had
pushed them even closer together. *She didn't know what she
would have done without him!*

"I'll go now, dear, since you're tired, but I'll be back tomorrow. I've cancelled my pupils this week." He opened his eyes. His mother looked tired herself. He wanted to say something to her but didn't know what to say. He'd already cut her off when she tried to talk to him. "Granny's coming too, and so is Andrea. Oh, and by the way, here are some cards for you." She took four envelopes from her bag and put them into his hands.

He read them after she had gone. There was one from Joe, and one from each of the Katy McIlroy trio. The pictures on the cards showed a selection of people and animals lying in hospital beds bandaged up to the ears.

Joe had written: 'You never do things by halves do you, Rembrandt? Take it easy in hospital now, right? Just lie there and be good. Cheers, Joe.'

Katy had written: 'Hope you're feeling better. We miss you. Love, Katy.'

Jane had written: 'We were terribly worried about you when you disappeared and searched all over. Get well soon. Love, Jane.'

Susan had written: 'I was very sorry to hear about your appendix. The party turned out pretty awful. Will tell you about it when you get out. Love, Susan.'

Nick put the four cards on top of his locker.

"Fan mail?" said John.

Nick grinned.

His grandmother arrived before his mother the following afternoon. She came with her knitting bag under one arm and a bagful of sustenance under the other. She did not trust hospital food.

"And how are you then, lad?" She dumped the bags and bent over to kiss him. Then she examined the chart at the bottom of his bed and shook her head as if she didn't believe any of it. After she had unpacked the contents of the food bag into his locker and poured him a glass of Lucozade – "Drink it up now, you've got to get your strength back!" – she settled herself on the creaking upright chair and began to knit. She was making him a slate-grey V-necked sweater which he would never wear. He hated grey, regarded it as a non-colour. But he found the presence of his grandmother strangely comforting, more than he did that of his mother who when she came was restless and kept fiddling with things on the window-sill and locker top. She seemed to have something – or someone – on her mind. Apart from the state of his health.

"Here comes Andrea," said Mrs McLintock, taking the piece of knitting and holding it across Nick's stomach. He felt like a prisoner, helpless, who had to submit to other people's hands. "I do believe you've grown every time I measure you."

"It's the bandages."

"Hi, idiot brother!" Andrea tossed a giant bar of chocolate and a paperback on to the bed and propped herself up on the end.

"Mind his scar now, Andrea!" said her grandmother.

"And I'm not sure you should be eating chocolate, Nick," said his mother.

"So how're you doing?" asked Andrea.

"I was out jogging this morning. Twice round the Meadows."

"Only twice! Tut, tut. You are slacking. Quite a family party eh?" said Andrea, reaching out to take a cluster of grapes from the locker. "Nothing like a good illness to bring out the relatives."

"Or a death," said Nick.

"I think you're looking remarkably well," said his mother. "Much better than yesterday."

"The doctor didn't like the look of my scar this morning."

"Didn't he? What was wrong with it?" Mrs Murray's brow puckered.

"Stop worrying, Mother!" said Andrea.

"You won't tell me when to stop worrying, Andrea!"

"No fighting over the top of my corpse," said Nick.

"You do like your little joke, don't you?" said his grandmother.

"I must go soon," said his mother. The roads were bad and the forecast had said there would be more snow later. "Are you coming, Andrea?"

"I thought I'd stay with Janey."

Mrs Murray made no attempt to dissuade her. Perhaps it suited her to have Andrea stay in town? That way she would be on her own with Ed Black. She said she would see Nick tomorrow.

"Will you be bringing Mr Black with you?" asked Mrs McLintock. "Since it's thanks to him that Nick got here in time."

"I don't know." Mrs Murray was intent on buttoning her coat. She ended up with one buttonhole left over and the coat hanging squint and had to start again. "It depends."

"On what?" said Andrea, spitting a grape stone into the palm of her hand. "If he's free? But he's always free. He's what you might call a man of leisure."

"All right for some," said Mrs McLintock, knitting furiously.

Nick was the only person in the group who was still.

"Goodbye then, dear," said his mother. A quick kiss on his forehead, and she was gone. She had not answered *her* mother's question.

"I'd like to meet your lodger one of these days," said Mrs McLintock.

"Good heavens, is that the time?" said Andrea, looking at her watch and springing up, setting the bed rocking.

"Is lover boy awaiting you in his chariot?" asked Nick.

His grandmother clucked reprovingly. The word lover she considered to be vulgar. She would have considered it even more vulgar if she had known he had used the word correctly. Andrea had to restrain herself from sticking out her tongue. Nick smiled at her. Being in a hospital bed had its own advantages.

He was left with his grandmother who knitted steadily on as the afternoon light waned behind the window and the tea trolley came and was cleared away again. Nick dozed off and on. Sometimes she talked, reminiscing about times she'd been in hospital herself; sometimes she was silent, lost in her knitting and her own thoughts. Somewhere in those thoughts Ed Black might lie.

"I was thinking," she said, as she rolled up her knitting and speared the ball of wool with the needles, "that when you get out of hospital you might like to come and spend a day or two with me before you go home?"

"Yes, I might, thanks, Gran," he said, surprising himself.

Chapter Nine

He saw more of his grandmother than of anyone else during the ten days that he was in hospital, apart from the nurses of course. She arrived every day at the start of afternoon visiting and stayed until it ended. She brought her knitting and enough food to keep the ward going.

And then one evening Ed turned up. Nick was startled when he saw him making his way towards him.

"I was in town this afternoon so thought I'd stay on and come and see you."

Nick mumbled something then occupied himself by taking a long drink from his grandmother's Lucozade. Over the rim of the glass he eyed his visitor who stood at the end of the bed looking uncertain as to whether he should go or stay.

"How are you feeling?"

"Much better thanks."

"Good."

A nurse whisking past said, "Is your visitor not going to sit down then, Nick?" And to Ed. "Might as well take the weight off your feet."

Ed still hesitated.

"Yes, do sit down," said Nick formally. He could hear his voice stiff and cold. Like an icicle.

Ed pulled up the chair but did not bring it too close to the bed.

"Is it still cold out?"

"Very. There was ice at the edge of the sea this morning."

"Was there?" Nick felt himself thaw a little. He wished he could have seen the ice. It was not often that the sea froze.

"You're certainly looking different from the last time I saw you!"

"Thanks for coming with me that night by the way."

"Think nothing of it. Accidents and illness – things

74

like that – don't bother me. I wanted to be a doctor when I was young. But there wasn't enough money for me to stay on at school." He spoke in a matter of fact way, uncomplaining.

"I keep telling Joe he should stay on at school and get some qualifications."

"You're dead right to tell him that. I will too when I see him."

"Do! He needs to be bullied." Nick grinned. He lay back against the pillow, slid down the bed a little. He was really quite pleased to see Ed, or would have been if it hadn't been for the other complication. But that complication would have to be put aside in the meantime. He did not feel strong enough to tackle it head on at the moment.

"Oh, I almost forgot." Ed put his hand into his pocket and pulled out a paperback book. "I saw this and thought you might be interested."

"David Hockney! Oh, I am. I think he's fantastic! Those paintings he's done of swimmers are just incredible." Nick opened the book, found a plate illustrating one of the paintings he'd been referring to. Le Plongeur. "Look! I wish I could see the real thing. I heard him on the telly one night saying that a painting was closer to the truth than a photograph. And it's true! He made me realise that."

Ed smiled at Nick's enthusiasm. "I'm glad I got it then," he said, nodding at the book. He pulled his chair in closer and together they looked through it, with Nick talking, enthusing, pointing things out.

"Looking at this makes me feel desperate to get back to painting again."

"You're lucky to have something you want to do so badly."

"Oh, I know."

"He lives in the States now, doesn't he? Hockney? In California."

"Does he?" said Nick, knowing that he did, since he had watched the television programme right through.

"Ever fancied going to America yourself?"

The question was not as simple as it sounded. Ed had asked casually enough but Nick sensed a more serious intention lying underneath.

"Not particularly," said Nick, closing Ed off. He collapsed against the pillow and yawned.

Ed said he'd be getting along.

"Thanks for coming. And thanks very much for the book."

"Don't mention it."

Ed looked back briefly from the door before he disappeared into the corridor.

Nick's fingers curled round the edge of the Hockney book. He wished he didn't like Ed as much as he did. He wished he hated him. It would be easier if he did. Ed was a threat to his father and his father was hundreds of miles away and unable to watch out for himself. He ought to be watching out for his father instead of hobnobbing with his rival and taking presents from him. He should have faced Ed with it tonight no matter how strong or weak he felt. What's going on between you and my mother? But how could you ask questions like that? Andrea might be able to; he couldn't. He lifted his hand and the book slid down the bedclothes on to the floor.

"You've dropped your book." The nurse bent down to lift it. She smoothed the cover and immediately he felt contrite to see the corners dented. She laid it on the locker top. "You look a bit flushed." She put her hand on his forehead. "What's been exciting you, Mr Nicholas Murray?"

"Hey, Rembrandt!"

Nick looked up from his book to see Joe grinning in the doorway.

"Joe! Come on in!"

"All right for you to have more than one visitor?"

Of course, he would be with Katy McIlroy! He didn't seem to be able to walk down the street without her any more.

"Yes, it's all right."

Joe disappeared and a second later was back leading the Katy McIlroy trio. Susan was carrying a box that had once been filled with chocolate bars and now bulged with an assortment of bags and tins.

"Looks like we're going to have a party," said John.

"How are you then?" the girls wanted to know as they clustered round Nick's bed. Joe thought he looked the picture of health and was just kidding on that he was ill so that he could lie in bed in the warm. It was perishing cold out, he said, the worst winter for years, and their pipes had burst and they had no running water. "I would just stay where you were if I was you."

"I'd like to see *you* lying in bed! They'd need to tie you down."

The girls shed their woollen hats and scarves and duffle coats and hoisted themselves up on to the bed saying they were fine and didn't need chairs. Joe took the chair in pride of place. He said he might as well, if nobody else wanted it. The Chief Visitor's chair, Nick called it.

"Now give us a blow by blow account of your operation," said Joe, "and then the girls'll distribute the refreshments."

"Well, they brought me in here and they got this carving knife as long as your arm and went slit, just here! Then they yanked all this stuff out, yards and yards of it —"

"Stop!" said Katy. "You're making me feel ill."

"Have a can of Coke," said Jane, reaching into the box for one.

"And a packet of crisps," said Susan. "Smoky bacon."

"And a spring roll," said Katy, lifting a greasy looking package which was still warm. "Fresh from the chipper down the street."

"They'll be taking your stomach out after all that lot," called over John who had no visitor that evening.

The girls included him in the hand-outs and soon he too was crunching the crisps and drinking Coke out of the can.

"So what happened to you at the party, Nick?" asked Jane. "When you disappeared?"

"I just crawled away home, I felt so bad. And what happened at the party after I left?"

"We had a bit of a dust up," said Joe, turning his face and pointing to his left eye which looked slightly puffy. He grinned. "We had some gatecrashers who didn't want to go away. They had to be persuaded."

"It was a disaster," said Katy with a sigh. "You should have heard my parents when they came home! The place was just about wrecked."

"And my father turned up in the middle of it all," said Jane. "They could hear the noise from the house. I've got to be in at nine now every night. Nine!"

"He'll change his mind, come Christmas," said Katy.

Christmas was coming, there were only fifteen shopping days left, and the shops were seething, said the girls; and the Christmas tree on the Mound was lit. Would Ed Black be away by Christmas? wondered Nick.

And then the girls began to talk about parties again. Nick couldn't believe it. After the last fiasco?

"If I have one in my house it won't be like that," said Susan. "My mother and father won't go out for a start."

Nick was glad that he would be convalescent: nobody could attack that excuse.

"How's the car going, Joe?" he asked when he got the chance to change the conversation.

"Haven't done anything on it recently. Too cold to work outside."

"And how's the scooter fund getting along?"

"Nowhere. I'm spending money like water these days."

On Katy, presumably.

"Still, you only live once," said Joe, with echoes of his mother. It was one of her favourite sayings.

Nick didn't see Sister coming. The girls were blocking his view of the doorway.

"And what's going on here?" she demanded.

The girls slid off the bed. Their boots had left grubby marks on the coverlet.

"You know you're only supposed to have two visitors at a time, Nicholas?"

"Two of them are mine, Sister," said John. "They live in my street."

She didn't believe a word of it, that you could see, but she didn't challenge him. She said that this was the noisiest room in the ward, if not the whole hospital, and departed, shaking her white starched hat. The girls clambered back up on to the bed.

"She's not a bad old stick, she just likes to sound off," said John. "Got any more of those salt and vinegar crisps, love?"

Katy tossed a packet over.

When they left, Nick's bed looked like a rugby team had had a workout on it, and he himself felt exhausted, sticky and overfed, but happy.

"Are you sure, now, that you want to go to your grandmother's?" asked his mother, who had come early, before her own mother, to ask the question.

"Quite sure."

"Fine. She'll take good care of you. And she'll enjoy having you."

So she was not going to try to talk him out of it, say that she'd prefer him to come home straightaway. She might prefer it if he went to live full time with his grandmother.

"There's a letter from Dad for you." She gave it to him. "I cabled him after your operation, just to tell him you'd had it and were okay. Aren't you going to read it?"

"I will later."

He waited until his grandmother had arrived and when she and his mother were engaged in conversation about some relative or other in Belfast he slit the edges of the airmail letter open with a pencil. He unfolded the blue sheet. Over the edge of it he saw that although his mother was still talking she was watching him.

'Sorry to hear about the appendix, old man,' his father had written. 'Though I expect by this time it'll be knitting up nicely and you'll soon be leaping about again. One thing about an appendix, you can do without it.'

"Hold my wool for me, Rona, will you?" said Mrs McLintock, slinging a skein of wool over her daughter's hands and beginning to wind it into a ball. I'd like to paint her winding wool, thought Nick, and went back to his letter.

'The job here is okay in itself, the kitchens are well-equipped and so forth, but living here is no fun. It might be all right if you were single but it's no life for a married man. I miss you all a heck of a lot, especially with the thought of Christmas coming. Sometimes I wonder if it's all worth it. I know the money's good but money's not everything.'

"What's your father got say for himself then?" asked his grandmother.

"Nothing much," said Nick, folding the letter, putting it away inside his locker.

Chapter Ten

The stairs leading up to his grandmother's flat seemed longer and steeper than he had remembered. He had to stop to recover his breath on the second landing.

'Are you all right, Nick?'' asked his mother anxiously, looking back.

"He's young," said his grandmother. "He'll soon get his strength back. Lying in bed softens the muscles."

They continued up the last flight in single file, his mother leading, his grandmother bringing up the rear. He had looked forward so much to this day of getting out of hospital and yet when it had come he had been sorry, too. Being in hospital had been a way of life, a quite enjoyable one, once the initial period of pain and misery had passed. And the problems of the outside world had seemed remote, as if they didn't really have all that much to do with him. Now, following his mother's heels, he thought of her returning home to Ed Black. And of his father sweating away in the Gulf, missing them.

"Nearly there," said his mother.

A last effort, and he made it to the top landing. His heart was pounding and his legs felt like jelly. Lying in bed, he had thought of jumping on his bicycle and cycling out to Joe's. He wondered if he would even be able to make it as far as the Sea View Café.

"Now what we all want is a nice cup of tea," said Mrs McLintock as soon as they were in the sitting room. She had a good fire going in the grate. Thick, dark tea and soft, floury scones bursting with currants. What with the tea and the heat of the fire, Nick thought he would go straight to sleep.

"Still got your lodger, Rona?" said Mrs McLintock, who asked the question every other day.

"Yes." Mrs Murray set down her cup and picked up her handbag. Two bright pink spots lit up her pale cheeks. "He'll be leaving soon though," she said hurriedly and began pulling on her coat. "I must go, I've got a pupil at three."

"When is he going?" asked Nick.

"Sometime before Christmas."

"Where? Baltimore?"

"Baltimore?" said Mrs McLintock. "Is he a travelling fella then?"

"No, he's changed his mind about America. He'll be going to Belfast to begin with." Mrs Murray was flustered now and couldn't find her gloves. "To spend Christmas with his family."

And then? wondered Nick. What then? He found his mother's gloves under her chair.

She kissed him, told him not to overdo things and she'd ring tonight to see how he was.

Nick and his grandmother listened to the ring of her feet going down the stone stair.

"Bit nervy these days, your mother, if you ask me. Maybe it's with your dad being away."

Nick made no comment. They heard the stair door bang at the bottom. He got up and went to the window to look down on the street. He saw his mother get into her small car which was spattered with mud and slush. It looked small three floors down, and so did she. She drove off carefully, between the ruts of snow.

"I've made up the bed-settee for you in here," said Mrs McLintock. "I thought it would be warmer and you can take a wee rest when you feel like it."

He was glad of that for the spare room was poky and dark and as you opened the door you could feel the chill striking you. He liked the idea of lying in bed with the firelight flickering over the walls.

His grandmother sat at one side of the fire knitting and he at the other sketching her.

"I don't know what you want to be drawing an old woman like me for!"

He smiled, carried on. The day passed in a comfortable,

nerveless sort of way, punctuated by cups of tea and idle conversation.

Andrea arrived in the late afternoon bringing a crackling nervous energy into the flat with her. She drank a cup of tea but would not eat any of the scones or coffee cake. She perched on the window ledge annoying her grandmother who preferred people to sit down properly in a room. Andrea wanted a cigarette, Nick could tell that. And she was het up about Carlo no doubt. Situation normal. What a waste of energy, he thought, as he shaded his grandmother's chin.

"And what about this fella Carl then?" said Mrs McLintock. "You've never really told me what he does."

"He's got a restaurant."

"A restaurant? What kind?"

"Just an ordinary one."

"I see," said Mrs McLintock, obviously not seeing the picture as clearly as she wished. She scratched the back of her head with her knitting needle. "Does he cook then or what?"

"He *can* cook but he's got a chef. He cooks when it's the chef's night off."

"And what sort of stuff does he cook?"

"Lamb, veal, chicken, in different sauces."

Nick remained silent. It would be more than his life was worth – and after his brush with death he considered it to be worth quite a lot – to open his mouth on this one.

"I saw Joe this morning," said Andrea, turning to him. "He was asking for you. Oh, and so was Susan."

They began to talk about school, about pupils and teachers and the play the dramatic society had chosen. Safe subjects. Subjects in which their grandmother had no interest. She began to nod off. Her hands slackened over the knitting needles, the ball of wool bounced down on to the floor, her chin drooped. Andrea signalled to Nick to follow her into the kitchen. She closed the door behind them.

"What is it, Andrey?"

"Mum."

"Mum?" He felt his stomach lurch and put a hand to his scar.

"I'm worried about her."

"Because of Ed?"

"So you've seen it too?"

"They seem to be very friendly."

He did not want to tell Andrea about the photograph, not yet at any rate, not until he had found out more about it himself. He was hopeful that he might. Through his grandmother.

"They're more than friendly – they're close. In the way that people are when they can understand what the other is thinking without having to say."

Was she like that with Carlo? Nick felt glum. The word, and the condition of glumness, filled his head. He wished he were back in hospital cracking jokes with John.

"But what can *we* do about it?"

"Nothing. I was thinking of writing to Dad but if I did Mum would never forgive me." Andrea sounded miserable. "It would be like telling tales behind her back. Betraying her. And I couldn't do that. Besides, it might not do any good, it might just push her further into Ed Black's arms."

Nick did not know what to say. This was an area about which he knew nothing. He listened to Andrea.

"Marriages break up all the time of course. Well, look at Mandy's Mum and Dad! They split last summer. He went off with a woman half his age and her Mum's miserable."

"They've always got on all right though haven't they?" Tiredness was beginning to sweep over him in waves. He would have to lie down soon. "Our parents?"

"I suppose so. Though they were arguing a lot before Dad went away."

"But we all argue!"

"The trouble is, Nick –" Andrea looked him in the eye – "I think she's in love with Ed."

Nick slept until the early evening and when he wakened he and his grandmother had a light meal and took their places at the fireside again. The curtains were drawn, his mother had already phoned, and no one else would ring the bell now.

"Can I have a look at your photographs, Gran?"

She was always pleased to have an excuse to take the old chocolate box out of the sideboard. She untied the faded blue ribbon that held it together. The box was filled to overflowing with pictures of the family in every stage of its development.

"Was that one taken in Ireland?" Nick pointed to his mother in a summer dress sitting on some rocks.

"That was the Giant's Causeway, at Portrush. And there she is on the sands at Bangor with my brothers."

"That was Great Uncle George wasn't it? On the right?"

"Yes, that was George." Mrs McLintock sighed. "Poor George. No one deserved an end like that. And here are my brothers walking on the Twelfth."

Nick looked at the two men, dark-suited, bowler-hatted and sashed, stepping out.

"We had some great days on the Twelfth, mind. All the bands playing and the flags flying and folk in the street waving. There were some good tunes. Did I ever sing 'The Sash' to you lad?" She hummed and then broke into the words.

'It is old but it is beautiful
And its colours they are fine.
'Twas worn at Derry, Aughrin,
Enniskillen and Boyne.'

And as she sang her foot tapped.

"But the Boyne was a long time ago, Gran! 1690 wasn't it? Why go on singing about it?"

"Why not, Nick? It's a part of our heritage. If it hadn't been for the Boyne and King Billy we wouldn't have been Protestants."

"Would it have mattered that much?"

"Indeed it would!"

85

"Honestly, Gran!"

"Honestly what, Nick? My religion *means* something to me. And why shouldn't it, tell me?"

"But if it divides people —" He stopped. He would get nowhere. "Let's have a look at some of the other photographs."

A lot of the photographs were of Nick's mother, but there was no replica of the one he had seen in Ed Black's suitcase.

"She was very pretty, Mum, wasn't she?"

"Very. Like Andrea. All the lads had an eye for her."

"Did she have many boyfriends? Before Dad?"

"I can't remember now." Mrs McLintock crammed the photographs into the box and pushed on the lid. Her mood had changed. "What about a cup of cocoa, son?"

"No thanks. I couldn't eat or drink anything more. Dad wasn't Mum's first boyfriend, was he?"

"I don't suppose he was."

"Oh come on Gran, tell me! There was someone else, wasn't there?"

"How do you know?" Her voice was sharp.

"Just guessing."

"What if there was?"

Nick went on, "Was he a Scot? Or did she meet him in Belfast?"

After a pause, Mrs McLintock said slowly, to herself more than to him, "Yes, she met him in Belfast." She seemed almost to have forgotten that he was there, and was so much inside her own thoughts that she had not registered that he had guessed too much, too easily.

"Was she — was she in love with him?"

"Seemed to be."

"What happened?" he prompted, quietly.

"They weren't suited."

"In what way?" There was no answer. She was gazing into the fire. "Was he a Catholic?"

"Yes!" She was back with him now, looking him straight in the face. He could see the indignation in her eye, even now, at the thought of her daughter walking out with a

Catholic boy. "I just couldn't understand it. And I never will."

"Was that why it broke up? Because he was a Catholic?"

"Of course."

"I wouldn't have thought Mum would have minded."

"*We* minded." Mrs McLintock looked up at the photographs on the mantelpiece, of her father who had been Worshipful Grand Master of his Orange Lodge, of her brothers who had followed in his footsteps, with sash, bowler hat and drum.

"Did she want to marry him?"

"There was some nonsense like that in her head for a bit."

"You stopped her?"

"She saw it would be no good."

"And did he too? The boy?"

"Oh yes, Eddie Doyle saw it was no use either."

Eddie Doyle.

"The Doyles were a bad lot," said his grandmother, back to talking to herself. "A right bad lot." Her voice had changed from being regretful, to being bitter. She shook herself. "Anyway, let's forget it, lad. I don't know what we had to get on to that subject for. It's all dead and buried, thank God, long, long ago."

Chapter Eleven

Coming home again after two weeks away – two weeks which on looking back seemed to have been more like two months – Nick saw everything in a different light. The bay, the terrace, his own house. It was like coming into a strange place. He went round looking at things, touching them.

"When something fairly traumatic happens to you," said his mother, "you often feel like that afterwards."

He saw Ed Black in a different light too. He no longer saw him as the lodger who had come in off the cold street one afternoon but as Eddie Doyle, a Catholic from Belfast who had been in love with his mother the daughter of his very Protestant grandmother and whose brother – surely Michael Doyle was some relative? – had killed his mother's Uncle George. The two events must be related even though they were separated by a number of years. Years meant nothing to the Irish. After all his grandmother talked about 1690 as if it was yesterday.

And Eddie Doyle was still in love with his mother: there was no doubt about that. Watching them together, Nick saw that he was, by the look in his eye and the softness of his voice when he spoke to her. And she? Was she in love still – or again – with Eddie Doyle? He could not be certain, that was more difficult to judge, for his mother was guarded, aware that she had two children in the house who were watching; but he suspected that she was. In Ed's company, she laughed, her eye brightened, and when they were alone in a room together they could be heard talking and talking.

Of course Nick had known – suspected anyway – that Ed Black must have been in love with his mother to have kept and carried her photograph around with him, but he had not allowed himself to put the thought into words, not even inside his own head. He sought out Andrea who was sitting at the desk in her window staring gloomily into the back garden.

"Andrea, about Mum and Ed –"

"I don't want to talk about it, Nick."

"But it was you that brought it up in the first place!"

"I know. But he's going away in a week."

And she had other things on her mind. She swivelled round in her seat.

"Carlo wants me to go to Rome with him for Christmas."

"And Mum won't let you?"

"She won't even listen! We'd be staying with relatives of his, millions of them, so it's not as if I'd be going away on my own with him. His mother will be there too. And you know what Italian mothers are like! She probably wouldn't even let us out of her sight."

"Doesn't she mind that you're not a Catholic?"

"Carlo says she'll accept that once she gets to know me. He's sure she'll like me." Andrea sounded desperate. "That's why it's so important for me to go, don't you see?"

Nick could see that it was if she and Carlo had planned to get married; not unless.

"Andrey, you shouldn't rush into anything, you know."

"I'm not rushing," she said impatiently. "I just want to go to Rome and meet Carlo's mother. Is that so unreasonable? And I want to be with Carlo. I'll die if I don't get to go!"

"You look too healthy to go into a decline."

"That's all you know. Wait till you fall in love! Though, knowing you, I doubt if you ever will."

Nick picked up a glass paperweight from her desk and, rotating it between his hands, gazed into the whirls of colour which were spun through the glass. He wished that his mother would let Andrea go to Rome, for with her gone, and Ed Black too, the house might settle down and become more peaceful for a while. He wished that Andrea would go to Rome and never come back. Ever.

"Nick?" Her voice was soft and wheedling now. "Would you talk to Mum for me?"

"Why me?"

"You are her favourite."

"That's not true!"

"She does listen to you."

"Don't involve me in this, Andrea."

"You never want to be involved in anything, do you. Go on, stand on the sidelines! That's you all over. And whenever anything difficult comes up you just retreat behind your easel."

Painting was not a way of retreating, he told her; it was a way of looking at the world and trying to record it. He put down the paperweight and banged the door behind him when he went out but her words, as they often did, had found their mark. Just as her words about doubting if he'd ever fall in love had. They scrabbled about in his head and would not lie down.

Next morning after Andrea had gone to school (he was not to return himself until next term), he broached the subject of Andrea going to Rome with his mother.

"I'm not even going to consider it," she said and ran water into the sink.

"But why?"

"I want Andrea to be home at Christmas. Especially with your father away. And I can't afford to give her any money."

"Carlo's going to pay her fare."

"I don't think he should."

"I don't see why he shouldn't. He won't be buying her with the ticket. You're just looking for excuses, aren't you?" Taking a drying up cloth, Nick stationed himself beside her.

"You know I don't care for Carlo and that I think he's far too old for her, apart from anything else."

"So what is the anything else?"

She was scattering a great deal of water around as she washed the dishes. She lifted her bent shoulders in a slight shrug. "He just doesn't seem suitable to me."

Nick picked up a clutch of wet knives. "But how can you judge who's right for Andrea?"

"I *am* her mother and as such am entitled to have an

opinion, and if she decided to marry Carlo I would feel I was lacking in my duty if I didn't try to persuade her not to. I can see the relationship much more objectively than she can. And I'm sure it wouldn't work."

"What would you have done if your parents had tried to talk you out of marrying someone you wanted to marry?" He had to work hard to control his voice and hold it steady.

Her hands ceased their hectic activity. She stood, bent over, her fingers submerged in the hot, soapy water. She could not answer the question and he had not the heart to ask it again. He dried the knives and dropped them into the drawer.

"What are you going to do today?" she asked, making an effort to sound bright again. "Paint?"

"Probably. But I thought I'd go along the beach first."

Wrap up well then, she said, and don't tire yourself. Yes, yes, he said, only half listening. After she had finished the dishes she went to her music room and began to play a piece by Beethoven that was quiet and haunting.

When Ed came downstairs to go for his morning walk, Nick asked if he could join him.

"Sure! I'd love to have your company."

The sun was out making the sea glitter, the air was fresh and invigorating. They dropped down on to the beach and walked towards the headland.

Nick waited until they were in the lea of the rocks, out of the full force of the wind. "What are you planning to do after you go to Belfast?" he asked. He had determined to be like Andrea, to ask questions straight out.

"I'm not sure. I may go to England. Look for a job there." A gull, woefully bedraggled, passed close over their heads. "The birds have been having a terrible winter." Ed watched it go.

"Why did you change your mind about going to the States?"

"I haven't altogether. I might still go. It depends."

On whether my mother will go with you? Could he ask that? Nick cleared his throat. It felt as though it were coated with sand. Ed was stooping to look at a dead bird washed up against the wrack. Nick supposed that, if he really wanted to get anywhere, to find out what exactly was going on, he ought to ask the question. He looked down at Ed's dark head. Ask him! He told himself. Ask him! He did not. Instead, he, too, bent down to look at the bird.

Mrs Plummer was standing outside her gate when they came up from the beach. She waved a blue airmail letter at Nick. He went forward to take it from her.

"The postman put this through my door by mistake this morning."

Nick thanked her and took the letter, turning it over in his hand. It was from his father. She would have examined it thoroughly, no doubt, during the time she had had it in her possession. Not that it would have revealed much to her, sealed all the way round as it was. She looked past Nick and let her gaze rest on Ed. Then she nodded and went back up the path into her own house.

"I have a feeling she doesn't care for me," said Ed cheerfully. "She put the evil eye on me the moment I walked into the café."

"I don't think she cares for anybody."

"Poor woman. She's to be pitied don't you think?"

Nick said he supposed so, though was not convinced. He gave the letter to his mother, then went up to his room feeling annoyed with himself. He should have pressed on with his questions and not drawn back. Andrea would say that was typical of him. He sat down at his desk to write a letter to his father but he could think of nothing satisfactory to say. His father seemed such a long way away. He wrote a line or two about the cold and the dead birds then gave up. And when he took up his paint brush he could get nowhere with that either. His hand was not in tune with his eye today. He threw down the brush in disgust.

He was pleased therefore when Joe came at lunchtime, even though he had the Katy McIlroy trio in tow. His mother and Ed were in the kitchen so he took his visitors up to his room where the girls pounced on his pictures and began exclaiming over them.

"This is a fantastic one of the shore," said Susan. "I really like this, Nick."

"Good. I'm glad you do."

"And look at Mrs Ramage and Mrs Plummer!"

"Gosh yes, old Plummer," said Jane giggling. "Thank goodness I don't have to go to her for piano lessons any more."

"This is good of Joe," said Katy, turning up the painting of Joe working on his car, with Nick watching.

Joe had lain down on Nick's bed, had his hands behind his head and was staring at the ceiling. He was behaving in a very un-Joe like manner. What could be up with him? He had the air of being preoccupied with other things, the way Andrea did when she was brooding over Carlo. Surely Joe was not brooding about Katy? After all she was here in the room with him talking twenty to the dozen and tossing her dark frizzy hair about.

"Yes, Rembrandt's really got what it takes," said Joe, turning his head. But he remained detached.

After school, he came back on his own. Nick, feeling apprehensive, made coffee and carried it upstairs. He waited for Joe to speak.

"Dad's got a new job."

"*No!* He can't have."

"He has. Starts after New Year."

"Where?"

"Southampton."

"But that's miles away." Nick sat down on the bed. Mr Marks couldn't be so selfish as to do this. Surely he couldn't!

"Four hundred," said Joe gloomily.

"But why?"

"You know Dad!"

"But what about your mother?"

"When it came to the bit she quite fancied a move too. Just when everything was going great for *me* here! I've liked this place better than any other place we've ever lived in."

"Then don't go! You've got your O grades coming up. You won't have much chance if you have to move schools in the middle of the year. Don't they see that?"

"Not really." Joe shrugged. "Dad says if I want to drive I can get on without them. The way he did."

"But didn't you tell him you might want to do other things?"

"Of course." Joe sounded weary. "They do want me to get on, you know. They're good to me but they're just – Well, they're just as they are and you can't do anything about that."

"No, I suppose not," said Nick, feeling calmer now. He had been thinking fast. It might be impossible to stop Mr and Mrs Marks from moving, but it might well be possible to stop Joe. "Come in after school again tomorrow."

At suppertime that evening Nick had little appetite.

"Aren't you going to eat any more than that, Nick?" said his mother.

"Got to build your strength up," said Ed.

He had managed to build up his and was a changed man from the one who had arrived looking haggard and drawn on a wet November afternoon. His cheeks were no longer sunken and he walked with a straight back and a firmer step.

Andrea had not much appetite either but her mother did not comment on that, knowing where it would lead. She did not have to give Andrea any excuse to raise the subject of Rome.

Mrs Murray took a dish of bread and butter pudding out of the oven.

"You can't expect me to eat that," said Andrea. "It's far too fattening."

"It's my favourite," said Ed.

Yes, thought Nick, it would be. Ed was the one in the house for whom his mother cooked now.

Andrea put her elbows on the table and rested her chin between her hands. In a very quiet voice she said, "I wish I could go. You've no idea how *much* I wish it. I wish it more than anything I've ever wished."

"It's out of the question, Andrea," said her mother. "And I don't want to hear any more about it! And that's final."

Andrea rushed from the room and went pounding up the stairs. She would throw herself on to her bed and weep.

"Poor girl," said Ed softly.

Mrs Murray did not meet his eye as she set his pudding in front of him.

Ed said he would wash up.

"Can I talk to you about something, Mum?" asked Nick. "In my room?"

She and Ed exchanged looks before she followed Nick out of the kitchen. She was clearly relieved when he began to talk about Joe and agreed at once that she didn't see why Joe shouldn't come and stay with them for six months so that he could finish his school year here.

"It does seem a shame that he should have to switch schools. The only thing is that I think I'd have to ask his parents to pay for his food."

Nick felt sure that would be all right. "They'd have to feed him anyway." And when the six months were up perhaps Joe would stay and do another year at school and take his Highers. He did not bring that up now. It was something that would probably happen naturally. His mother liked Joe, she would not want him to leave.

"I thought he could have Ed's room."

"Ed's?"

"He's going, isn't he?"

"Yes, of course." She nodded, as if she were reminding herself. "I'd have to ask Andrea if it is all right with her too."

"She doesn't care about anything except Rome at the moment."

"Please don't mention the word in my hearing again, Nick!"

"Sorry!"

She really was on edge. When Joe came they would be able to ignore all these upheavals, they could go out on their bikes together, or sit in one or other of their rooms and drink coffee, play records, talk. There was the Katy McIlroy trio of course but he was prepared to put up with them as long as Joe didn't have to go away.

Andrea said it was all one to her who came to stay in the house.

The following afternoon, Nick put the proposition to Joe.

"Are you serious? Have me to stay for six months?" Joe looked startled. The idea had obviously not occurred to him. "Your mother wouldn't mind?"

"No, honestly." Nick laughed. "We often have lodgers anyway. So what do you say?"

"Well, I don't know. I mean I don't know if my parents'd go for it or not."

"They've got to, Joe! You're sixteen now. You can choose for yourself, can't you?"

"I suppose so," said Joe dubiously. "I'll need to talk it over with them though."

"Shall I get my Mum to ring yours, to reassure her that it's all right?"

"Okay," said Joe. His brow was creased with a frown.

Mrs Murray rang Mrs Marks and they had a long talk. Nick, hovering on the upstairs landing, heard his mother say they'd love to have Joe, he was just like one of the family and he and Nick got on so well, and it seemed a pity for Joe not to have a chance to do his exams here, and the English exam system was quite different, so she believed. "It would be no trouble at all to have him, Mrs Marks."

"Thanks," said Nick, when he went downstairs. He gave her a hug. "What did she say?"

"She thanked me and said that if he was to stay she'd be very happy for him to stay with us. But she'd prefer him to go with them."

"But that's not fair to Joe!"

"She said they wouldn't make him go. It would be up to him to decide."

Chapter Twelve

"It's difficult," said Joe.

"But you want to stay, don't you?"

"Yes, I do. Very much."

"Well then?"

They were in Nick's room. Joe was sitting on the window sill, playing absentmindedly with his pocket knife, opening the blade and pulling it out and shutting it again. Nick had never seen him so fidgety.

"Well, it's my mum really." Joe shut the knife and held it clasped in his right hand. "She'd miss me, I know she would. You see my dad's away such a lot and she'd be on her own."

"But she *wants* to move doesn't she? Your dad wouldn't have taken the job if she hadn't agreed?" Nick felt outraged at the thought of Mrs Marks's selfishness. They might at least have waited six months. Or she might, and gone later. "You're sixteen. She can't expect to keep you at home for ever."

"She doesn't. Another year or two and I'll be off and she knows it. Suppose that's why she doesn't want me to go too soon."

"Why *doesn't* she follow your father in six months' time?"

"Because we've never lived that way. She's always gone with him."

"But he's away half the time anyway."

"I know. But she doesn't see it that way."

Nick thought it was as well he was not strong enough yet to cycle out to Joe's house. If he were he would be tempted to go and give her a good shaking and say, "Let Joe off the hook! He wants off. You're being so unfair to him."

Joe put the knife away, slid off the sill. "Let's go and see if the girls are in the café."

They were drinking coffee, and looking miserable. Susan and Jane perked up when the boys came in but Katy's smile was watery. The fizz had gone out of her.

"What's going on in here?" said Mario. "Is it a wake or something?"

"Joe's going away," said Katy limply.

"Now I haven't decided yet," said Joe.

"You *can't* go," said Susan.

"We won't let you," said Jane. "We'll tie you down."

Katy was silent.

"What would you do in a new place?" said Susan.

"You wouldn't know a soul," said Jane.

He might make new friends, thought Nick, though at sixteen it wouldn't be so easy. People had their friendships formed by that age, especially at school. But was that really true? For hadn't *he* made new friends recently? They were here right now – the Katy McIlroy trio. He had to admit that they had become friends. And it would be awful to think that one wouldn't go on making new friendships as life moved on. But he didn't want Joe to move on and make a new life that excluded them. And nor did Joe. That was the unfair thing about it.

"Come on, Rembrandt, waken up!" Joe elbowed him. "It's time for us to leave you and head back up the hill."

"I'll go with you to the gate."

Joe walked ahead with Katy, as was their habit, and Nick came behind with Susan and Jane. Katy was doing plenty of talking now. She was talking passionately, turning inwards to speak directly to Joe's face.

"Surely he wouldn't go and leave Katy," said Jane.

"You'd miss him a lot too wouldn't you?" said Susan to Nick.

Nick nodded.

"You'll come to my party on Saturday won't you?" said Susan.

Nick started dissembling saying he wasn't sure, he didn't think he was up to a party, not yet, he got tired after he'd been standing for a while and his scar began to hurt. He felt like an old woman offering excuses. Susan said he didn't need to stand, he could sit in a corner.

"It's just a small party. Only about twenty."

Twenty sounded like a lot of people to him. He said he'd think about it.

"Do you always have to think about things?" demanded Susan.

"I suppose I do," he said, feeling slightly huffed.

"Katy and I are going to call for you on our way past," said Jane. "So we won't be taking no as an answer."

How determined the three of them were! He hoped their determination might wear down Joe's reservations about letting his parents go without him. He said as much to his mother when he came home.

"I wouldn't put too much pressure on Joe if I were you, Nick. He needs to be left alone to think. Decisions like that aren't easy. I'm sure he's confused and pulled both ways."

Was she confused and pulled both ways? But she shouldn't be! She was married to his father. Shouldn't? What did he know about it to say that she shouldn't be confused? After all, she had once been in love with Ed Black. Before she met his father. Ed Black alias Eddie Doyle had come first. Nick's head ached.

His mother said he was looking pale and suggested he lie down for a bit. But he was too restless to lie in bed; he'd done enough of that in the last couple of weeks. He went out again, pottered a little way along the beach, but the wind from the sea was cold and he did not feel too good so he went up on to the promenade and back along to the café thinking to pass a half hour or so with Mario talking about things that had nothing at all to do with the matters which were gnawing away inside his head.

But Mario was not alone. Seated at the counter drinking a cup of coffee and smoking a cigarette was Carlo. He must have parked his car round the corner.

"Hello there, Nick. How're you keeping now? Better? Good. Another cup of coffee, Mario."

Mario set a cup on the counter and Nick, somewhat unwillingly, perched on the stool next to Carlo.

"I'm just on my way along to see your mother."

"Oh," said Nick, not asking about what, having no need to.

Carlo finished his coffee, stubbed out his cigarette and leapt to his feet brushing off his blue velvet shoulders. "Wish me luck!" he said to Mario.

Mario said nothing until his brother had left the café. "I think your mother is right, you know. Better to marry one of your own."

"One of your own what?"

"Kind! Well, Carlo would do better to marry a Catholic girl when he comes to marry. Of course he would! Then they would worship at the same church, bring their children up together in the same faith. That way no battles, no pulling in different directions." Mario looked over his shoulder at the picture of his wife and four children propped up on the shelf in front of the biscuits. "Marriage is tricky enough without having other complications."

Nick could see that.

"Would your mother be against Carlo marrying Andrea?"

"She would certainly not be for. She has a very lovely girl picked out for him in Rome. The daughter of a close friend. The match would be ideal."

Whereas a match between Andrea and Carlo would be considered as far from ideal by the families on both sides. Even the wedding itself would be a trial, with Carlo's Roman mother brought together with their Belfast grandmother. Nick grinned at the thought of it.

"I have nothing against Andrea herself, you understand," said Mario.

"Except that she is not Italian and not Roman Catholic?"

"She will find another young man. Younger, more suitable."

The door jangled open and Mrs Ramage entered. She came straight up to the counter taking the stool Carlo had vacated.

"Mrs Plummer's just gone off to Edinburgh on the bus," she said to Mario. She leant forward and lowered her voice even though the only other person within earshot was Nick who could not fail to hear what she said no matter how low she said it. "She had a box under her arm. She's away to sell her mother's china, I'm sure of it." Now she turned to look at Nick. "She's really feeling the pinch."

"Everybody's struggling these days," said Mario, giving his counter a thorough wipe. "Could she not get help from Social Security?"

"Social Security? Ada Plummer? You must be joking!"

Nick slid from his stool. It seemed there was no peace to be found anywhere today, neither inside his own house nor outside it. But before he reached his gate Carlo came out of the front door. The interview had been short, and obviously not sweet.

"Mothers!" he said to Nick as they passed.

Mrs Murray and Ed were talking in the kitchen and the door was not properly closed. Nick stood in the hall taking off his anorak. They were so absorbed in their conversation that they had not heard him come in.

"But, Rona, Andrea goes to university in the autumn and in another couple of years Nick'll be off to college too."

Nick froze.

"So you can't let them influence your decision can you, not really . . ?"

Kicking his anorak into a corner, he ran up the stairs and into his room. He closed the curtains, lay down on the bed. Soon he must confront his mother, ask her some questions, but not yet, not this afternoon, whilst his head was beating as if in time to a Lambeg drum. He closed his eyes and slept and dreamt of those enormous drums playing for an Orange walk on the twelfth of July: he saw the men of the Lodges marching, bowler-hatted and sashed, keeping time to the music; he saw the banners flying LONG LIVE KING BILLY; he saw his great-uncles step down out of their photograph on his grandmother's mantelpiece and stride forward to confront a man standing on the sidelines and although he could not see the man's face he knew that it would be Ed Black alias Eddie Doyle who was in love with his mother who was married to his father who was

101

sweating in the Persian Gulf and whose sweat was breaking out on his own forehead. And then he saw Joe in the middle of the throng burling round and round and round, his arms outstretched as he tried to find something to hold on to. Nick awoke with a jerk to feel a hand on his forehead. For a moment he thought it was the hand of his great-uncle George dead from an IRA bullet and he cried out, "Leave go of me!"

"It's all right, lad," said Ed. "You've been having a nightmare. And you've cooked up a bit of a temperature from the feel of you. Overdoing things I expect. Here's your mother with the thermometer."

His temperature was up and she wanted to call the doctor but he persuaded her not to. Ed backed him up. "A bit of a rest and he'll probably be all right." Nick promised to take things easy for a few days. He only wanted to be left alone, and not to be fussed over.

Ed came in later and took his temperature again. "It's going down. I thought it would." He shook down the mercury. "I'm going in the morning, Nick. I'll be away early so I'll say cheerio just now and have a good Christmas when it comes."

"And the same to you."

Ed looked back from the door. "Expect I'll be seeing you again," he said.

Nick stayed in bed for most of the next day, came down in the evening for their meal.

"Well, just the three of us again," said Mrs Murray dishing up and trying to sound cheerful. She didn't look very cheerful. And neither did Andrea who was making no effort to conceal it.

"Don't give me much. I feel sick."

"Your father's sent money for your Christmas presents," said their mother, ignoring Andrea's remark. "Got any idea of what you'd like to have from him?" As she spoke of their father her face showed no emotion.

Susan came along on Saturday morning to see if Nick

would be fit enough to come to the party.

"I think you could go, Nick," said his mother. "At least for a little while. It would do you good to have a change and it's not as if you've far to come home if you do feel ill."

Nick shuddered, remembering the last party he had come home from feeling ill.

Susan's house was decorated for Christmas: streamers pinned at the corners crisscrossed the rooms, coloured bells hung from the light fittings, pieces of mistletoe dangled from the doorways, the tree glittered in the window.

"It looks great."

"Thank you!" said Susan.

"Got you!" cried Katy, whirling him round and planting a kiss on his mouth. He looked up, saw white waxy berries above his head. And then he was being kissed by Jane and Susan and Eileen and Hazel. He felt dizzy.

"Just stand there all night, Rembrandt," said Joe. "You're doing all right."

"Come and have some food," said Susan.

Susan's mother was much in evidence in the kitchen. She was a large lady with strong forearms. She stood at the table cutting up quiche and dishing out salad. There was going to be no trouble in her house tonight.

The music had to be kept to a reasonable level too, for the sake of the neighbours. Nick, for one, did not mind: at least you could hear yourself speak. It was an easy-going, low-keyed party, and he felt himself relax.

"I'm glad you came," said Susan.

So was he, though he could not bring himself to say so. She was waiting, hoping that he would: he saw that, and yet could not say it. The directness of her gaze made him feel uncomfortable.

"I'll need to be going soon," he said.

"Suit yourself!" She turned away to speak to someone else.

He would wait a few more minutes and then slip away. Joe had spent most of the evening with Katy in a corner, talking. They liked to dance; usually neither could sit still.

Their faces were serious.

Jane came to sit beside Nick.

"I'm sorry I can't dance," he said, still keeping his eye on Joe and Katy. They were getting up now and beginning to move in time to the music. How easy it must be if you were like Joe!

"That's all right. You wouldn't want to burst your scar, would you?"

Joe and Katy were dancing wholeheartedly, Katy's black mop of hair was flying. When they reached Nick, they stopped in front of him.

"He's made up his mind, Nick," said Katy, unable to keep the smile from her face.

"Have you?" Nick looked at Joe.

Joe nodded. "I'm going to stay, Rembrandt. That's if you think you can put up with me?"

Chapter Thirteen

Mrs McLintock arrived on Christmas morning, in good time for lunch. She was brought by friends who were visiting relatives in the district. She admired the Christmas tree which Nick had decorated in silver, red and white, and she read all the cards which her daughter and grandchildren had received, both the printed messages and the written ones.

"I see you have one or two wee girlfriends, Nick," she said after she had read aloud, " 'Love from Katy', 'Lots of love from Susan', and 'Love and best wishes for the New Year from Jane'."

"He's a dark horse is our Nicholas," said Andrea, who had not put on the mantelpiece her card from Carlo. He had given her a silver necklet and bracelet before he left for Rome. Every now and then she raised her arm so that she could gaze at the bracelet with pleasure and with sorrow.

They had a glass of sherry before lunch.

"To absent friends." Mrs McLintock raised her glass.

"To Dad," said Andrea, with a glance at her mother.

"Dad," echoed Nick.

"To Dennis," said their mother and drank, though what she thought or felt they could not tell.

They ate in the dining room which, not having been used since summer, was a little chilly. Mrs McLintock kept on her hat and scarf. She had a hearty appetite and ate all that was set before her.

"So you've lost your lodger, have you?" she said, as she held out her plate for a second helping of turkey.

"Yes," said Mrs Murray quickly and concentrated on the carving.

"He's gone over to Belfast to see his mum," said Andrea.

Mrs McLintock looked pensive. "I envy him in a way. Going to Belfast, I mean, not to see his mum." She chuckled.

"I shouldn't think you'd care for his mother somehow," said Nick.

"What a funny thing to say, Nick," said his mother.

"Is it?"

"He's odd, that boy," said Andrea. "Shall I refill the glasses?"

"Please, darling," said her mother, whose eye was on her son and not her daughter.

I have her worried, thought Nick; she thinks I know something, which of course I do.

"Talking of lodgers," said Mrs Murray, "we're going to be having Nick's friend Joe staying with us for the next six months."

"That'll be nice for you, Nick," said his grandmother, though her mind was still on Belfast. "You know, Rona, I wouldn't mind going back to the old place, just for a short visit, to see everybody. It's been a long time."

"I thought you said you never wanted to set foot on the place again?" said Andrea.

"You feel like that after something bad happens but now . . . well, time's going on and I'm not getting any younger. Perhaps the bad memories fade a bit."

"What about you, Mum?" said Nick. "Would you want to go back? Or do you have bad memories too?"

She gave some non-commital answer then changed the conversation, assisted by her mother. They talked with determination about the quality of the present turkey and the one they'd had last year and the one they'd had the year before that. As they ate and drank the temperature of the room seemed to rise. Mrs McLintock was persuaded to take off her felt hat and replace it with a purple paper one shaped like a crown.

"I must say I do like a good family Christmas. It's a pity your father couldn't have been with us, when all's said and done."

"It is isn't it?" said Andrea.

At that moment the telephone began to ring and thinking perhaps that it might be Carlo calling from Rome, Andrea

106

reached for the door and dived into the hall. A few seconds later she was back, looking dejected. "It's for you, Mum."

"Me?"

"It's Ed."

"Ed?" said Mrs McLintock, dropping her knife and fork on to her plate with a clatter.

"Mr Black, the lodger," said Mrs Murray, as she hurried out.

"Ed," repeated Mrs McLintock. "I never knew that was his Christian name. It couldn't be . . . " She frowned, shook her head and the purple crown tumbled forward on her forehead. "No, of course it couldn't."

"Couldn't be whom, Gran?" said Andrea.

"Nobody, dear." Mrs McLintock straightened her hat.

Mrs Murray did not return to the dining room immediately after replacing the receiver. They heard her go into the kitchen. Andrea called out asking if she wanted any help and her mother called back, no, she was just getting the pudding out and everything was under control.

"Here we are!" she said, as she carried in the pudding burning with a weak bluish flame, and would have gone on to talk about Christmas puddings past and present if Andrea had not cut across to ask,

"And how is Ed?"

"Fine. Wishes you all a Happy Christmas. Pass the plates please, dear."

"Is he coming back?" asked Nick.

"He's not sure."

And there the topic of the lodger was allowed to rest.

"What about you doing some of the dishes, Andrea?" said her mother, when they had eaten until they could eat no more.

"I will, in a minute. I've got to phone Mandy first. I promised I would."

"I'll give you a hand, Rona," said Mrs McLintock. "It'll do me good to move about for a bit."

"I'll dry," said Nick.

"Can't you just leave them?" demanded Andrea, flaring.

"I've said I'd do them, haven't I? It doesn't have to be just this second." She departed upstairs.

"Bit jumpy, isn't she?" said her grandmother. "Is it that Carl fella? What's he like anyway, Rona?"

"I hardly know him. You go on out, Nick, and get some colour in those cheeks."

After eating so much, Nick was glad of the fresh air and exercise. He went down to the beach. The tide was out, the sand stretched smooth and wet to meet the green white-flecked sea. At the rocks he met Susan who had also come out to walk off her dinner. She was wearing a pale yellow knitted hat and long scarf to match. The scarf fluttered behind her like a pennant. I could paint her like that, thought Nick: laughing into the wind with the yellow scarf flying.

"Fancy walking round to the headland?" she said.

"All right."

He fell into step beside her. They talked about Joe and both expressed relief that he was staying and agreed that it wouldn't be the same without him.

In the early evening Mrs McLintock was collected and driven back to Edinburgh.

"See you bring your young man to visit me now," she said to Andrea before she left.

"All right," said Andrea.

"You wouldn't want to give her a heart attack, would you?" said Nick.

Andrea made a face at him, pulled on her wellingtons and went out to visit Mandy.

Mrs Murray withdrew to her room and put a piece of music on the record player. Nick stood for a few minutes in the hall listening to Mozart's flute concerto then went resolutely up the stairs to confront her.

"I have to talk to you about Ed."

"All right, Nick," she said quietly and turned down the sound.

"Or perhaps I should call him Eddie Doyle?"

"Perhaps you should sit down first. It's easier to talk when you're on the level with someone."

Nick sat, on the other side of the fireplace. The log fire was shooting sparks half way up the chimney. He waited, letting her take her time. She sighed, asked how he had come to know about Eddie Doyle. He told her.

"Tell me the rest now though, will you?"

She nodded. "It started when I was fourteen and Ed fifteen. Yes, we were that young."

"Fifteen. That's the age I am now!"

"But Ed had had a different sort of life, he'd left school, was working. He was the eldest son in a pretty poor Catholic family."

"How did you meet?"

"Accidentally. On Albert Bridge. I was standing looking at the ships. So was he. We got talking. He lived near my grandmother, though not in the same street. We used to go over every year, as you know. We kept bumping into one another that summer and next. And when we were sixteen and seventeen we began to meet secretly, in strange districts, on the other side of town, in cafés, cinemas, going in separately, meeting up inside."

"Sounds like an awful lot of trouble to me."

She laughed. "But we were in love, Nick!" Her face was alight as she remembered. "And I suppose because it was forbidden it was part of the excitement. Then when we were older, seventeen, eighteen, we would go away for a day out of town, to Bangor or Portrush. I became an expert at making up alibis."

"For Gran?"

"Even more for *my* grandmother. You might think your grandmother is a staunch Protestant but she's nothing compared to what her mother was! As far as she was concerned the Pope was worse than the devil."

"How long did it last – you and Ed?"

"Until I was twenty and he twenty-one."

Six years. Nick bent down to put back a log which had tumbled out of the grate. Six years was a long time. They must have been serious about one another.

"We planned to marry. He was going to come over to Scotland."

"Gran said that you saw it would be no good?"

"It wasn't quite like that." Her face darkened. "We became careless, Ed and I. We were seen. My uncles went after him one dark night to convince him it would be no good. They left him unconscious."

"No!"

"He was in hospital for a week. You can still see some of the marks on his face, faint scars round the hairline."

"But didn't his family go to the police?"

"They didn't want that kind of trouble. But they sent a message to my mother. 'Take your daughter home before we do to her what your family has done to our son.' We sailed on the boat that night."

Now Nick needed to be silent to digest what his mother had told him. He saw her face as it had been in Ed's photograph, young, pretty, smiling, and then he saw the smile fade to be replaced by a look of pain and suffering.

"I'm sorry," he said.

"I didn't see Ed again for twenty years. Until that day in November when he walked in."

"So in between you married Dad –"

"And had you and Andrea."

"But you didn't forget him?"

"I couldn't. How could I, Nick, after all that happened between us? And that wasn't all. The IRA gunman who shot my Uncle George was Ed's brother."

Nick nodded. "I'd already worked that out. Was it a reprisal?"

"Partly, I suppose. Perhaps it was that if he was looking for a target my Uncle George was an obvious choice. The Doyles hated him, as you might imagine."

"But Ed wasn't a member of the IRA?"

"No, never. He was as shocked by the killing as everyone else was."

"Why did he come here?"

"He wanted to see me again. It's as simple as that. His wife was dead, he was free –"

"But you are not!" cried Nick.

She did not answer.

She could be free if she wanted to be: Nick knew that. People did get divorced, all the time, as Andrea had said.

"Do you – do you like him a lot then?" He had really wanted to say 'love', but had found the word too difficult to get out.

"Ed? Yes. I think I always will, no matter what happens."

"And Dad? What about Dad?"

"I love him too."

"But you can't –"

"Love them both? Why not? In different ways. It's difficult for you to understand, Nick, but you must see that both of these men have played a big part in my life."

Yes, he could see that, and he could see too that Ed Black alias Eddie Doyle had been there first and it might be that it would be that which would sway her in the end. Not only that: Ed had suffered on account of her. And she had suffered on account of him. That might be the biggest bond. His mind shifted from his mother to Ed, to Andrea and Carlo. He frowned.

"Mum, what about Carlo?"

"What about him?" By the look in her eye he saw that she knew where he was leading.

"He's Catholic too. Is that why you've been against him?"

She took a moment to answer. "I have to admit I didn't consider it a point in his favour."

"But *why?* When you should have understood."

"Perhaps it was because I understood too much. It opened up old wounds, Nick, can't you see? I couldn't believe it when Andrea brought him home the first time.

I didn't want her to go through what I did."

"But this isn't Northern Ireland! And I'm hardly likely to beat Carlo up." That made her smile.

"There would still have been your grandmother to contend with. So, okay, we could have coped with that. I know she can't be allowed to influence Andrea's life. But where emotions are concerned, Nick, one is not always very logical."

"You can't go on being against Carlo now though, can you, not for that reason?"

"No, you're right, I can't."

"You must tell Andrea. About yourself and Ed and Uncle George and everything."

"I will. Probably I should have told you both before but I couldn't bear to speak of it."

"And now? What now?"

"I have a decision to make. And there's something else I must tell you – about your father and me. We hadn't been getting on at all well for some time before he went away – you must have realised that? – and in fact that was why he went. We agreed to have a year's separation and see how we both felt at the end of it."

Chapter Fourteen

Ed Black came back to the town three days after New Year. Nick was standing at the counter of the Sea View Café when he saw him go past carrying his cheap suitcase and plastic flight bag, and a fan-shaped bouquet of flowers wrapped in paper.

"Is that not your Irish lodger?" said Mario, craning his neck.

Mrs Plummer and Mrs Ramage, who were at their table having morning coffee, also looked round and then back at Nick.

"Looked like him." Nick lifted his bar of chocolate from the counter. "See you!"

Before he reached the door the women had started up.

"Didn't expect to see *him* back."

"Neither did I, I must admit, Ada."

"Wonder what he *does* want here . . . "

Nick closed the door on the buzz of their voices but was left with their words in his head. He knew what Ed wanted, but would he get it?

He let himself into the house. He stood still. His mother and Ed were in the music room talking in hushed voices.

Quickly, Nick went down the hall into the kitchen where Andrea was sitting at the table writing a letter. She covered the letter with her forearm as he came in.

"He's back."

"Carlo?" Colour rushed into her cheeks and her head swung up.

"No. Ed!"

"Oh, is he?" Andrea's head drooped again. "I'd kind of hoped he wouldn't –"

"I know, so had I."

"It's not that I don't like him. I do, and if it weren't for Dad –"

"But there *is* Dad."

"Yes, but maybe Mum and Ed would be better suited to

one another, Nick. Just because we're in favour of her staying with Dad doesn't mean it'd be the best thing for her."

Now Nick felt thoroughly depressed. The same thoughts had come into his mind but he had not wanted to acknowledge them.

"I mean, Ed *was* her first love," said Andrea.

As Carlo was hers. And she wanted to hang desperately on to the idea that first love was the best love. That first love could survive against the odds. She had not heard from Carlo since he had returned from Italy two days before and was convinced that he had met another woman, Italian, more mature, Roman Catholic. Nick had not told her about the lovely girl his mother had picked out for him in Rome. The ideal match.

"Do you think I should ring him?"

"Who? Dad?"

"No, stupid! Carlo, of course. Why *hasn't* he phoned me? He always used to every day. Without fail."

"You'd think you'd never heard of women's lib. You're not supposed to sit around pining for a man."

"I am *not* pining. And it's got nothing to do with women's lib. You are so thick at times, Nick Murray! You know nothing at all about relationships."

With that last thrust, she flounced from the room. No other word would describe the way she went. Thick indeed! Maybe he knew more about relationships than she thought.

She had forgotten in her annoyance to cover her letter. He inclined his head.

'I know that you think I'm too young for you and that worries you but I'm growing all the time and the age gap between us is getting smaller. Please don't stay away because of anything my mother said to you. Or because of anything your mother said to you. Don't let them come between us.'

When Andrea returned, Nick seized the kettle and turned on the tap. He gazed out into the garden at the black tree. That buds would ever spring again from those

114

bare branches seemed an incredible idea. The tree looked dead. Andrea had snatched up the letter and torn it into strips. Now she was tearing those into smaller pieces until they resembled confetti. Later, when Mrs Murray wanted to know what all the mess was, Nick said that Andrea had been playing at weddings and immediately felt horribly mean. Why did he have to say things like that? He had hurt Andrea when he had only meant to tease her and now she was running out of the room shouting that she hated him and he was an inhuman beast.

"Did you have to?" said his mother.

"I suppose not."

"Go upstairs and tell her you're sorry."

"She wouldn't listen. She'll just scream at me."

"Go on! Go and try!"

He went as far as her door, put his hand on the knob, withdrew it, and retreated to his own room. He sat down at his desk, picked up his ink pen and drew a little cartoon of himself, looking very thin and dark and dejected, with a bubble coming out of his mouth saying: 'I am an idiot. Please forgive me or I shall die of a bleeding heart.' Then he took the piece of paper and slid it under Andrea's door.

"You *are* an idiot," she said, on coming down for lunch; but she had forgiven him. She had cheered up too, though why, Nick could not fathom. Perhaps the cry she had had in her room had cleared her head. The swing of her moods amazed him. She talked cheerfully to Ed and he to her, mostly about some film or other that had been on television. Nick and his mother were quiet, speaking only when spoken to.

"Fantastic soup, Rona," said Ed. "I missed it when I was away."

"Doesn't your mother make good nourishing soup?" said Andrea.

"Not as good as this."

They smiled. Nick saw they would get on all right living together, Ed and Andrea; if they had to.

When the telephone rang Nick was glad of an excuse to

leave the kitchen for a few minutes. He found it difficult to look at Ed directly, or to talk naturally with him.

"Hello there, lad, how are you?" said his grandmother.

"Fine."

"And what's new with you?"

He hesitated. No, there was nothing to be gained, perhaps everything to be lost, by involving his grandmother in this. "Nothing," he said. "We're just eating."

"In that case I won't keep you. You might tell your mother to give me a ring later."

After Nick had replaced the receiver he kept his hand on it for a moment, thinking. He hadn't seen or heard of Joe for two or three days. He dialled the number. Joe himself answered.

"Where have you been keeping yourself?"

"I've been busy. Helping the folks pack up. They're off this Friday."

Nick was about to say he could take a run out that way this afternoon – he was fit enough to cycle again – when Mrs Marks called to Joe in the background and Joe said he'd better go, his mother had a drawer stuck half in, half out. "She needs my beef. I'll ring you later, Rembrandt."

Nick felt a little uneasy. Something in Joe's voice had been different. Or was he letting his imagination loop the loop again? He tried to shrug off the feeling of unease but remained restless and after lunch got out his bicycle and cycled aimlessly around the town not knowing which direction to take.

At a T-junction he met Susan, on her bike. "I'm just going out to see Katy."

"I'll ride with you, if you like."

"Okay."

The country roads had some icy patches; they had to go carefully. Susan's mother hadn't wanted her to go out on her bike. "I had to promise to cycle at two miles an hour and stop when a car comes." Nick smiled.

Katy was pleased to see them. "Have you seen Joe?" she asked Nick at once.

"Haven't you?"

"Not since Hogmanay. Maybe he's just gone off me."

"Don't be silly," said Susan. "He's busy, you know he is."

"But I could've helped. I offered."

"I expect he's a bit uptight at the moment," said Susan. "At the thought of splitting up from his family."

"But he's not really splitting up, is he? He's just going to stay at Nick's for six months."

"But his mother's making him feel he's splitting the family up."

"Exactly!" said Nick. That *was* the nub of the problem.

Joe did not ring that evening, as promised, and was not in school the next day, the first of the new term. Nick walked down the hill to the shop with the girls.

"They'll still be packing," said Jane. "I wouldn't worry if I was you, Katy."

"Nick," said Katy, catching hold of his arm, "would you go out and see him this afternoon after school? Please! I don't like to."

He promised that he would, even though he would have preferred not to. If they were still arguing and Mrs Marks was looking reproachfully at Joe, he would prefer not to be around. Mrs Marks might even turn on him, might even blame him. He was absentminded in class for the rest of the morning.

"Miles away as usual, Murray," said the maths teacher.

At lunchtime, an air mail letter was lying on the mantelpiece. "From Dad? Can I read it?" He stretched out his hand.

"Not this time, Nick, if you don't mind," said his mother.

Andrea raised an eyebrow. She had come home for lunch and was pleasing her mother by drinking soup and eating a little bread and cheese. She sat slouched over the table, her face pallid, the skin round her eyes tinged with blue.

"How was school?" asked Mrs Murray.

"Same as usual." Nick kept his eye on the letter. "Except for Joe not being there."

"What are you working on just now?" asked Ed.

"Nothing. I can't seem to think about painting at the moment."

"That won't last for long," said his mother confidently.

"I'm sure it won't," said Ed.

"Was that not the bell?" said Andrea.

Grumbling, Nick got up to answer it. Why could Andrea not go sometimes? She protested that she did, often.

Standing on the doorstep, wearing a brown velvet suit, slapping his arms about to keep warm, was Carlo.

"Is Andrea in? I went up to the café she usually goes to at lunchtime but I couldn't find her."

Nick flung open the kitchen door and announced, "A visitor for you, Andrea! From the Eternal City."

He had to press himself against the wall to let her pass. She rushed into Carlo's arms. Nick heard Carlo say, "I tried to stay away, I thought it would be best, but I couldn't," before he closed the kitchen door.

"Somehow I'd got round to the idea that we wouldn't be seeing him again," said Nick. "Perhaps it was just wishful thinking."

"Shush," said his mother.

Andrea came back briefly to say that she had two free periods that afternoon and was going into Edinburgh with Carlo. Colour had flooded back into her cheeks, her eyes shone. She hugged her mother and seized her moth-eaten fur coat from the cupboard.

"But, Andrea –" began Mrs Murray.

But Andrea was gone.

"She seems happy at any rate," said Ed.

"I still don't like him very much but I suppose I'll just have to leave it to them to sort out for themselves now."

"I somehow think you will, Rona. She might not even want to marry him."

She might well not, thought Nick, now that she was going to be left alone to make up her own mind. On the other hand, she might. Who knew what Andrea would do? He had always thought he could tell which way her mind was working but now he realised that a large part of her was a mystery to him. And that in spite of the fact that they'd lived under the same roof for fifteen years. How could you ever know for certain what was going on in another person's mind?

He desperately wanted to know what was going on in Joe's.

In the dwindling light Nick rode into the hinterland, passing the dark brown field where he had watched the lime green tractor work, and the road turning that led to Katy's house. It would be dark by the time he cycled back.

The curtains of the Marks's cottage were drawn back, the lights were on. Joe's car was gone from the far side of the house. Parking his bicycle, glancing in, Nick saw that the rooms already had an unlived-in look, even though the furniture was still there. Tea chests and boxes stood stacked against the walls, bare light bulbs hung from the ceilings.

Joe came to the door. "Rembrandt! Come on in!"

"What's happened to your car?"

"Farmer's let me lay it up in a shed." He led the way into the kitchen. "Mum's up at the house just now. Cup of coffee?"

"You're going with them, aren't you, Joe?"

Joe sat down. He looked across the narrow table at Nick. "Yes, I'm going. I know you're going to be annoyed with me and I don't blame you –"

"Not annoyed. Just – well, disappointed."

"I'm sorry, Rembrandt."

"It doesn't matter about *me* being disappointed – it's you. It's you that's got to leave everybody, change schools –" But even as he was talking, Nick knew that what he was saying was not strictly true. He *was* concerned about himself, he was thinking about missing Joe. A big black hole was opening up in front of him.

"I know all that. But when it came to the bit, seeing

119

them pack up , it really came home to me. I feel I should go with them, Nick. We can still keep in touch."

"How? Over four hundred miles? Bit far for an afternoon cycle run."

"I'll write, honest I will! Cross my heart. And I'll call you up on the phone from time to time, cheap rate. And I'll come back in the summer. Farmer's offered me a job."

"Maybe," said Nick. He felt dulled, as if someone had struck him on the back of the head. "You think you will but you'll probably have changed your mind by then."

"I won't," said Joe fiercely, banging his fist on the table. "I *want* to come back."

"You've always said that when you move on you never look back."

"That was how it used to be. But this has been different, don't you see? We can stay mates. A few hundred miles won't get in my way. And what's to stop you coming down at Easter to visit me?"

Quite a lot, thought Nick. For a start, he was not sure that he would fancy a holiday under Mrs Marks's new roof, and to be going on with, his mother might have gone off with Ed Black by then.

"What's to stop you, Rembrandt? Nothing. Not if you want to come. Say you'll come! Come on, say it before I sock you one!"

Nick grinned – he had to, Joe looked so fierce. "Well, I'm not sure, Joe, it depends –"

"On what?"

"A number of things."

Joe groaned. "You know, Rembrandt, you can be like an unmovable lump of stone at times."

"Immovable."

"You see! I'll never get that O grade English."

Nick left before Mrs Marks returned. He didn't want to have to set eyes on the woman, or speak to her. The words he would like to say would either stick in his throat or else come flying out like bullets. He left without making any promises about Easter. He said he'd have to see how things went.

He and Joe did not say goodbye. "Good luck in the new place!" said Nick. "I'll phone you next week," said Joe. "And write to me! Draw me cartoons, anything! So hang in there, Rembrandt, and I'll see you in Southampton." He had said he would go over to Katy's house later on to break the news to her.

Light flakes of snow were beginning to fall as Nick reached the outskirts of the town. They danced under the street lights. The shops had closed, the streets were virtually deserted. He cycled down the High Street, rounded the corner into Sea View Terrace and went on past number five to Susan's house.

She was upset to hear about Joe. "But I guess we can't do anything about it, can we?"

"No, nothing. We did all we could." Nick was aware of the bitterness in his voice.

"I'm sure we'll see him again though, Nick."

He shrugged. "Who knows?"

"You feel wounded by Joe's decision, don't you?" said his mother. "You feel Joe's let you down?"

"A bit, I suppose." Yes, a lot! One hell of a lot.

"Sometimes one has to let somebody down when one takes a decision." She paused, went on, "Friendships *can* be kept over a distance, if one makes an effort. And some friendships seem to stay no matter what you do in between and when you meet again it's just as it always was. Perhaps it'll be that way for you and Joe."

He did not want to talk about himself and Joe, not any more. He said, "Was it like that for you and Ed?"

"No, hardly. That is something different altogether."

Mrs Murray got up and pulled the curtains, blotting out the night. Nick watched her closely, saw her hesitate before she turned back in to the room and him. She was getting ready to tell him about her own decision. His father's letter had been brought upstairs, was lying on the low table in front of the fire.

"Your father's coming home at the end of the month."

"He's quitting the job?"

"He's already given in his notice."

Nick felt the tug of conflicting emotions: of pleasure and disappointment. Pleasure at the thought of seeing his father again so soon, disappointment that he had not been able to stay longer with this job.

"Grandmother McLintock will have plenty to say."

"Then she'll just have to say it. And the others. They can all say what they like."

Nick nodded.

"Someone wrote to your father, about Ed."

"It wasn't me!"

"I didn't think it was. Or Andrea either."

"Or Gran? Would she –"

"She wouldn't have known the address. Anyway, the letter was sent anonymously, and that's not your grandmother's style."

Suddenly he remembered the look in Mrs Plummer's eye when she handed him the letter from his father. "Mrs Plummer! She could have made a note of Dad's address when she got your letter by mistake." Instinctively, Nick knew his guess was right. People *could* sometimes be read, he thought, bemused by the idea. And as a painter he wanted to be able to read people.

"She's waited a long time to find a way to make trouble for me," said his mother. "And when she did it's proved to be more of a help than a hindrance. It's helped bring matters to a head."

She came back to her seat, and leant forward to sweep fallen ash from the hearth. Her face was flushed, but it had lost its troubled look now that she had made her decision. As Nick himself knew it was when you didn't now how to make up your mind that you felt torn apart. His mother straightened her back.

"Nick, I'm glad your father's coming back."

"Yes? His heart was thudding.

"Yes. When I read his letter I realised that I did want him to, that I'd been missing him. So, okay, he's not what my mother would call a good husband, he's not a good provider, but *I* can provide and he's a splendid cook and the paying guests love him. And *I* love him."

"It's not what people do – earning money and the like – is it, that makes you fond of them?"

Mrs Murray smiled. "That's quite true, Nick."

"Now take Gran –"

"With her prejudices?"

"Yes. I feel I shouldn't even *like* her. Life muddles me at times."

"Not only you!"

"And Ed, what about him?"

The telephone rang in the hall below.

"Blast it!" said Nick and ran down to answer it.

Andrea was on the line. Trust her! She always knew how to pick her moment.

"Would you tell Mum I'm going to spend the night at Janey's?"

"Oh, all right!" He wasted no more words, replaced the receiver and climbed the stairs again, moving more slowly than he had coming down, thinking now of Ed up in the attic room alone. He went back into his mother's room and closed the door.

"What *about* Ed, Mum? You said –"

"Yes, I know." She sighed. "And it's true – I do care for him a great deal and I always shall, even if I never see him again."

And she won't, thought Nick. It would be too difficult for her, and for Ed.

"Poor Ed," he said.

"Yes, poor Ed. He's had a bad deal in life. But I can't compensate for that, Nick. And I can't compensate for what my uncles did to him twenty years ago. Nor would he expect me to."

"Have you told him?"

"Yes. He's going in the morning. To look for work somewhere in England."

Nick listened to the strong, sure sound of the sea and

wondered if Ed did, too. The tide had been full in earlier and would be receding again. Ed was quiet overhead. Nick imagined him setting out in the morning carrying the cheap suitcase and plastic flight bag, passing the Sea View café and the watching swivelling eyes, catching the bus into Edinburgh. From there a train would carry him southwards to some unknown place where he would have to start again amongst strangers. He would unpack the suitcase and bag in a strange cold room and walk down the street to buy his supper in the nearest chip shop.

Joe was going out, too, amongst strangers, but Joe was young and had his parents.

"I hope Ed finds something, Mum. Somebody."

"So do I! I expect he will. He's a strong man. And a resilient one. He doesn't take his knocks lying down. I'm glad he came back though, Nick, and that we had a chance to spend some time together and be friends. It's helped clear away those bitter memories. They'd eaten into me for years."

"Does he feel that way too?"

"Yes, I think he does."

They were quiet for a moment and then Nick said, "I think I'll go up and have a word with him."

"Do that. I'd like you to."

Ed was sitting by the window with the curtain drawn back. He had been looking out into the night. There was no moon, the sea was black. The street light illuminated the road, the sea wall. Nick pulled up a chair.

"I'm sorry you're going away, Ed. Though I've got to admit that I'm glad my father's coming back."

"That's only natural."

"It's funny how you can be sad about one thing and happy about another at the same time."

"Life seems to have a habit of working out that way. Or so I've found."

"You don't seem to have much to feel happy about at the moment."

124

"I wouldn't say that. I'm glad the old wounds have been healed between your mother and me. And I'm glad I got the chance to know you, Nick. I've enjoyed that."

"I have too. Though I think I could have been nicer to you at times. Like when you came to the hospital –"

"Ach, don't talk daft! I understood what you were going through."

That was what Nick liked about Ed so much: he understood; but not only that, he accepted, without bitterness. Nick looked round. By the door stood the suitcase and flight bag already packed. He hated the thought of Ed unpacking them in a strange room. He hated the thought of Ed being amongst strangers.

"We could still be friends, Ed, if you'd like to be. I would."

"And so would I! I'd like it very much indeed. I tell you what, Nick – when I get settled I'll write to you, will I?"

"Please! And I'll write back."

"And maybe you could come and visit me one day. I could always give you a stretch of floor to doss down on."

"I might come at Easter," said Nick slowly. "I'm thinking of going south at Easter."

"That'd be great! That's only three months away. Where are you planning on going?"

"Southampton."

"Ah. To visit Joe?"

"Yes. I'll definitely be going, Ed – I've just made up my mind – so you can count on a visit from me."

"I'll have something to look forward to then."

"So will I." Nick stood up. "I'll see you before you go in the morning."

He walked down the two flights of stairs and – picking up his anorak on the way – out into the night. He crossed the road and dropped over the sea wall on to the damp sand. Through the darkness he saw the white edge of the waves. Their sound filled his ears and their spray touched his face.

Turning his back to the sea, he surveyed the street and its houses. Tomorrow he would start on a new painting, a large one, of the terrace at night. He would paint the rectangles of light which broke the dark, larger rectangle of the terrace into patterns. He would paint the moon-shaped face of Mrs Plummer at her window peering out into the street. He would paint the Sea View Café shuttered and dark and place the short stocky figure of Mario outside it watching the sea and puffing a fat cigar. He would paint a long low red car rounding the corner with the dark head of Carlo in the driver's seat, and the fair one of Andrea beside it. He would paint the house at the other end of the terrace where Susan's family lived, with all its lights lit up like a ship at sea, and he would paint Susan herself standing on the pathway with her yellow hat and her yellow scarf fluttering like a pennant. And in the centre of the picture he would paint number seven, his own house, with his mother's room lit but the curtains drawn back, and her face at the window too, like Mrs Plummer's, yet so unlike Mrs Plummer's. Her face would be happy and sad at the same time. And on the pavement below he would paint his father.

His imagination stood still then. How would he paint his father? He could not get a clear picture in his mind of his father. But perhaps he could not expect to, not yet, not now, after so much had happened. After his father had returned and their lives had resettled then he would be able to see how to paint him. He might even paint himself. Where should he be? And what would he be doing? He would have to think about that. There would be plenty of time for that central part of the picture to take shape. He would leave it until last. He would start on the easier parts: the rectangles, Susan with her yellow hat, Mrs Plummer at her window, Mario holding a glowing cigar.

He began to walk. He would begin in the morning, after Ed had gone for the bus. Such a painting would be a big undertaking and might take months to complete – it would be what was known as a major work – but he would persist and work on each section until he had put on the canvas exactly what he saw in his mind's eye.